BELLA

Notte

Beautiful Night

by

HEATHER GRAY

BELLA NOTTE
Beautiful Night
A Tuscan Legacy ~ Book 6

© 2018 by Heather Gray

ISBN: 978-0-9981423-3-3

Contact Information: heather@heathergraywriting.com

Cover Art by Marion Ueckermann: www.marionueckermann.net

Cover Image Background ID 92602052 Adobe Stock © Photocreo Bednarek
Cover Image Sunflower ID 54536334 Adobe Stock © Miroslawa Drozdowski
Cover Image Man ID 53708428 Adobe Stock © Viorel Sima
Cover Image Woman ID 54446028 Adobe Stock © Syda Productions
Scene Breaker Sunflower ID 76249464 Adobe Stock © Cobalt

Eight grandchildren—one legacy!

When Isabella Rossi invites each of her adult grandchildren to her estate in the Tuscan hills for her eightieth birthday, she hopes to reunite a family fractured by distance, death, and secrets.

The birthday gift of a painting, arriving unsigned and with no sender's details, rips open old heartbreak. One family secret has already been revealed, her youngest son Albertino's illegitimate English daughter. Now it seems there could be yet more secrets.

Returning home, the cousins scattered across three continents each discover their lifetime love. When they gather again at the villa as summer ends, the remaining secrets are revealed. But can they be forgiven, or will the mistakes of the past be repeated?

This nine-book Christian romance series from seven of your favorite authors releases weekly from April 2018. Each novella is a complete and satisfying romance, filled with faith, family, forgiveness and love. Begin your journey to Tuscany this summer with Book 1 of A Tuscan Legacy!

Please visit us at underlineatuscanlegacy.com.

FAMILY TREE

A Tuscan Legacy

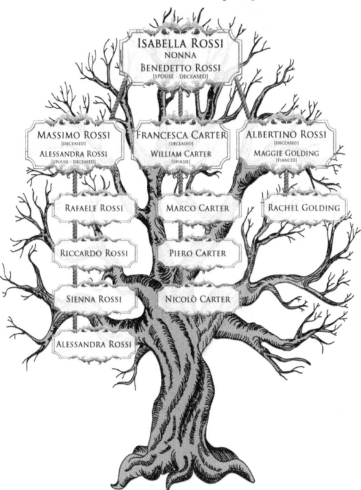

ISABELLA ROSSI
NONNA
BENEDETTO ROSSI
[SPOUSE - DECEASED]

MASSIMO ROSSI
[DECEASED]
ALESSANDRA ROSSI
[SPOUSE - DECEASED]

FRANCESCA CARTER
[DECEASED]
WILLIAM CARTER
[SPOUSE]

ALBERTINO ROSSI
[DECEASED]
MAGGIE GOLDING
[FIANCÉE]

RAFAELE ROSSI

MARCO CARTER

RACHEL GOLDING

RICCARDO ROSSI

PIERO CARTER

SIENNA ROSSI

NICOLÒ CARTER

ALESSANDRA ROSSI

TUSCAN LEGACY

THAT'S AMORE
Book 1 by Marion Ueckermann

LUNA ROSA
Book 2 by Elizabeth Maddrey

RAPSODIA
Book 3 by Alexa Verde

TI AMO
Book 4 by Marion Ueckermann

LA FIAMMA SACRA
Book 5 by Clare Revell

BELLA NOTTE
Book 6 by Heather Gray

SOLO TU
Book 7 by Narelle Atkins

DOLCE VITA
Book 8 by Autumn Macarthur

LA RISPOSTA
Book 9 by Autumn Macarthur

in celebration of my Savior
in memory of my daughter
with pride in my son
with gratitude for my husband

GLOSSARY

Italian

buongiorno — good morning
caro cugino — dear cousin
mi bella dama — my fair lady
nel suo cuore — in his heart
stupido — stupid

French

Basilique du Sacré-Cœur — Basilica of the Sacred Heart
Bassin de la Villette — The Villette Basin
café crème, s'il vous plaît — coffee with cream/milk, please
Cimetière du Père Lachaise — Père Lachaise Cemetery
je vous en prie — don't mention it
mademoiselle — miss
Marché aux Puces — Flea Market
merci — thank you

monsieur — mister
Musée d'Orsay — Orsay Museum
Musée des Égouts — Museum of the Sewers
Musée Rodin — Rodin Museum
numéro de chambre — room number
Place des Vosges — Vosges Square
vous désirez — what would you like

Then the LORD God said, "It is not good that the man should be alone; I will make him a helper fit for him.

Genesis 2:18

CHAPTER ONE

PIERO CARTER RAN AS IF his life depended on it.

Between the idiosyncrasies of German traffic and his cab's flat tire, he was late.

Beyond late.

He was the photographer, and the photo shoot couldn't very well start without him. No worries there. He prided himself on a level of professionalism, even if it had deserted him at the moment.

Ha.

It hadn't deserted him. It had ground him under its heels and left him like a pile of dust.

His destination was in sight through the next doorway, and Piero sprinted for it.

He didn't plan for the slippery rug, though. Or the curvy blonde who stepped into his path.

He went down hard, and he took the woman with him.

At least he managed to land under her. That had to count for something.

The rug they were on — acting more like a flying carpet than a proper historic replica — carried them through the entryway before it skidded to a stop at the foot of the famed English Stairway, one of the gems of the Dresden Royal Palace and the site of that day's photo shoot.

"Uh-hem."

Marty, the assistant assigned him for this shoot, stood by with arms crossed and eyebrows raised. "So nice of you to join us, Mr. Carter. We might actually be able to start this shoot before the lighting is completely ruined."

Good ol' Marty. He made obnoxious people look like sweet-tempered, little old ladies.

The blonde, who hadn't screamed even once as they'd careened across centuries-old wooden floors, jumped from his lap as though she'd been given a good jolt of electricity. Her face flamed red as she sent him a glare before she scuttled across the room and behind the temporary curtains set up to create a pseudo-dressing room for the models.

Not that models tended to be particularly modest. But it was generally bad form to wander around historic landmarks in a foreign land when wearing nothing but skivvies. Or less.

Piero shook off the shock of his grand entrance and made his way over to the camera table. He'd set it up the day before, double-checked all his settings, and arranged each camera the way he liked it. Not that he was fanatical… After all, he'd only requested one security guard to keep an eye on the shoot site overnight.

He ran his fingers along the cameras as he contemplated the stairway and the light filtering through the windows. His eyes flitted over to the curtained-off area.

Just who had that woman been?

Piero shook the thought away and picked up the camera he wanted. A quick turn on his heel had him facing the waiting crowd.

"Alright ladies! If you don't already know what you're doing, see Charise. She'll tell you when you're up."

The woman in question shook her silver-topped head, a smile dancing in her eyes. Then she clapped her hands, drawing the models' attention. "Analise, you're up first. Next is Patrice. Then Genevieve. You do not step in front of that camera until I've approved your outfit and makeup. Understood?"

The models all nodded but remained more or less motionless, except for Analise. A nod from Charise, and the young model was climbing the steps. She turned to face Piero as Charise's assistants worked to drape her dress just so. A whistle from their boss told the assistants when their work was done. They flitted to and fro to get out of the way. Some went up the stairs, and some went down. Better to separate than to risk tripping over a dress's fabric and undoing the work they'd already put into creating the perfect image.

Piero paced back and forth at the foot of the stairs as he looked at the model, the empty space, and the shadows.

He took a couple of test shots before calling for a shift in two of the reflective umbrellas.

It was going to be a long day.

His head wasn't in the game. He couldn't rid himself of the feel of the blonde in his arms. As soon as he'd gone down and taken her with him, he'd wrapped his arms around her. Instinct had taken over, and he'd wanted to protect her from further harm.

Instinct didn't explain the jolt he'd felt. Or the way she'd fit into his arms as if she'd been made just for that purpose. Or the way her softness had felt perfect against the sharp angles of his body.

He would have to track her down later and apologize. Maybe he could get her name, offer to buy her dinner.

She was only half of his distraction today, though.

Italy.

His family.

Nonna.

Nothing was ever going to be the same. He had a cousin he'd never heard of, and something was afoot at Villa Rossi.

Nope. Nothing was ever going to be the same.

Charise's clap brought Piero back to the present.

The model now climbing the stairs was... Who was she? That wasn't Patrice or Genevieve. Had they already gone through the first three models?

"Makeup!" Charise's voice boomed in the marbled space.

The blonde shot out from behind the curtain, a bag over her shoulder. She stopped by Charise, listened, and then climbed the stairs with purpose in each step. She had to squeeze up tight against the banister and rise up on her tiptoes to move around the dress's fabric, but she did so with agility. One arm looped around the banister, she used her free hand to pull something out of her bag, and then leaned precariously over the dress's extravagant train to dab something on the model's face.

When Charise whistled, the blonde pulled herself back to the relative security of the banister and tip-toed her way back down the steps.

Not before Piero's finger slipped on the shutter button and captured her image. A couple of times.

He might need the image so he could find her to make his apology. When he thought about it that way, *not* taking her picture would be downright rude.

Besides, he was a photographer. Taking pictures was simply what he did.

It had nothing to do with the way her hair caught and reflected the sunlight like liquid gold, or a desire to see what color her eyes were. Blue? Or grey? He couldn't tell from this distance. Nor was it about the way she bit her bottom lip as she concentrated —

whether on doing her job or on keeping her balance, he couldn't tell.

And it wasn't about the electricity that had started zipping through him again the second she'd appeared from behind those curtains.

Nope. It definitely wasn't about that.

CHAPTER TWO

FELICITY SANK INTO THE STEAMING water of the bubble-filled tub.

Ahhh.

She'd earned the bath.

A long, grueling day of running hither and yon to meet Charise's demands was par for the course.

Starting that day pitching foot-first across the floor in front of the entire crew? Not so much.

She already felt like a lump of coal next to the trim, graceful, and chic models. But this morning? Felicity couldn't have been any more gauche if she'd tried.

Someone knocked on the hotel room door.

If she ignored them, they'd go away.

Bdt-bdt-bdt. The door had a vaguely hollow sound to it, which only served to emphasize Felicity's annoyance at being disturbed.

The person at the door wasn't leaving. And now they were pounding hard enough to make the door rattle in its frame.

One of the models probably wanted her to do a quick makeup job before a night on the town. If that was the case and she ignored the door, she'd hear about it the next day.

Felicity pulled herself from the tub, her muscles protesting with every move. She grabbed the hotel's cotton robe, wrapped it around herself, and tied off the belt.

A headache started to throb at the base of her skull as she peered through the peep hole.

Flowers?

Must have gotten the wrong room.

She released the safety latch and pulled the door open.

"Delivery for Felicity von Wolff."

She blinked at the two-foot-wide spray of flowers between her and the voice. "You must be mistaken."

The bouquet moved to the side, and a man's face appeared. "Delivery for Felicity von Wolff, room 1822."

"That's me, but…"

He shoved the flowers through the door. It was either grab onto the mirrored vase or let the whole thing go crashing to the floor.

Felicity backed into her room so she could put the bouquet down.

The door swung closed as soon as she let go of it.

He had to be used to that sort of thing in hotels, though. Surely he'd still be there waiting for his tip when she opened the door again…

She pulled her purse from the closet and yanked a twenty euro note from her wallet. Was that a fair tip? Too much?

Tipping at a restaurant she could handle. Flowers, though? She didn't have any practice in that department.

Felicity pulled the door back open. The man was still there. He wasn't reaching for his tip, though. He was handing her a box wrapped in the signature copper foil of Germany's premiere chocolatier.

Oh, dear.

Flowers *and* chocolate? Twenty euros probably wasn't enough of a tip.

The box now clutched to her chest, Felicity tried to talk to the man. "Can you tell me who sent them?"

He smiled. "Felicity von Wolff, room 1822."

"Yes, that's me. But where did the flowers and chocolate come from?"

His smile didn't waver. "Felicity von Wolff, room 1822."

"You don't speak English, do you?"

He nodded.

She handed him the twenty euro note.

He turned and jogged down the hallway, passing three different models as he went.

"Holy cow, Felicity!" Patrice squinted over the makeup artist's shoulder. "Did you finally start putting out? That's one doozy of a bouquet."

Felicity offered the best smile she could muster. "He didn't speak English."

Patrice hooted. "The guy you put out for or the one who delivered the flowers?"

Heat climbed Felicity's chest, and she snugged the robe's belt tighter. "Har-dee-har-har."

Patrice caught her eye. "You know I'm joking, right? We all know you're not that kind of girl."

"Yeah. Too uptight for that," one of the other models called out before slipping back into her room and shutting her door with a bang.

Patrice nodded toward the closed door. "Ignore her. She's jealous, that's all. And any girl who doesn't mind hanging halfway across a stairwell with nothing but her elbow hooked around a banister to keep her from tumbling down the steps isn't uptight. No worries there."

What was she supposed to say to that? Patrice seemed nice enough, but women turned catty so easily. It was hard to know who to trust. "Thanks."

The model's smile seemed genuine, though. "Go on. You still have bubbles clinging to your hair. Get back in your tub. And eat an extra piece of chocolate for me since I won't be able to touch the stuff till after this shoot's over."

Felicity backed into her room and closed the door quietly. She slipped the security latch into place before walking over to the flowers. The bouquet sat on the low-slung dresser. It blocked the television, but she didn't really have any other place to put it. Besides, she wasn't up on her German well enough to watch TV anyway.

The bouquet was an explosion of color with bright pink Mokara orchids, red gerbera daisies, breathtaking coral roses, and yellow calla lilies — all interspersed with deep purple hydrangea and a handful of other flowers she couldn't identify.

Wow.

She unwrapped the chocolates and opened the box. The candies were nestled in a molded holder and surrounded by iridescent tissue paper. She popped one into her mouth and savored the delicacy for a second before searching for a card.

Nothing on or in the box of chocolates gave anything away. Finally, at the very back of the bouquet, she found a small card tucked into the plastic pick shaped like a devil's fork.

Apologies for today's wipe-out. I hope you'll let me make it up to you. Piero

Hmph.

Flowers and candy from Piero the Playboy.

The plastic pick snapped in two.

She pulled another chocolate from the box and dropped the two pieces of the pick into the garbage can nearly hidden at the end of the dresser.

Piero was a jerk, plain and simple.

She'd been on shoots with him before. He went through women like water through a sieve — fast and indiscriminately.

Except for one thing. He didn't date women like her.

She had too many curves, and she covered the ones she had.

Make it up to her?

Sure. If he could tell her where they'd been the first time the two of them had been assigned to the same shoot.

Ha. Not likely. She'd bet money — but not chocolate — that he hadn't even known her name until today. And even then, he would have had to ask someone.

Felicity yanked two more chocolates from the box and headed back to her bubble bath.

If anyone else knocked at her door, they could stand out there in the hallway until she was good and ready to open it.

Which would be never.

CHAPTER THREE

PIERO ARRIVED AT DRESDEN'S ROYAL Palace with time to spare.

No traffic catastrophes, no oversleeping, and no flat tires.

And all he needed to make the morning even better was for one Felicity von Wolff to show up. After the flowers and chocolates, she was bound to say yes to dinner. What woman could resist?

He was taking another turn around the courtyard, the site of that day's shoot, when a flash of movement caught his eye.

Sure enough. Felicity bustled across the expansive space, her hair in an up-do and unadorned.

He moved to intercept.

"I wanted to apologize again…"

"No." She cut him off.

"What?"

"No. Whatever you're selling, I don't want it."

Maybe she'd hit her head during yesterday's tumble. "I'm not selling anything."

She finally looked him in the eye, but her gaze gave nothing away.

Piero tried again. "I was hoping you'd let me make it up to you by taking you out for dinner."

The line of her mouth teetered on the precipice between grim and menacing. "I have no intention of being one of your conquests, Piero Carter."

He took a step back.

The fisted hands resting on her hips were the only indication of how she felt. Her voice, in contrast, raised by not even a single decibel. "You date a different woman every other day. You never stick around. As soon as you get what you want, you move on. When you run out of models, you go after the local talent. Whatever actress or musician happens to be nearby."

He took another step back. Is that what people thought of him?

"I have no intention of being your next conquest."

"I…"

"Yesterday's forgiven. Water under the bridge. No harm, no foul. Whatever." An edge creeped into that previously even voice. "But if you keep harassing me, yesterday's *wipe-out*, as you so aptly put it, will be the least of your worries."

Felicity walked away before he could form a coherent thought, let alone put it into words.

His phone vibrated. He pulled it out of its holster and glanced at the message. The group text with his cousins and brothers.

His cousin Ric had received a painting for his birthday the day before. Anonymously, it seemed.

The cousins had all chimed in one at a time to say they hadn't sent it. Which, of course, led to the next question. If not them, then *who*?

Ric had sent pics the night before. The style of his mystery painting was hauntingly similar to the one Nonna had received for *her* birthday.

The whole thing was the kind of eerie that ranked as slightly-more-than-creepy.

Just what Piero needed at the moment. Nothing said *uncomplicated life* like a family conspiracy.

He could barely figure out his own life. He wasn't equipped to tackle the mystery of the paintings and contribute anything useful.

He tapped *Ignore* and slipped the phone back into its place.

"Alright ladies!" Charise clapped her hands to call everyone to attention.

It was going to be another long day if he didn't find the razor-sharp focus for which he was known.

"Hey, Piero." One of the models — Marli? Carli? — ran a finger down his arm. "I was thinking about going clubbing later. Want to go with me?"

A quick half-step put him out of her reach. "Afraid not, doll. Catch me another day."

Her lips formed a sultry pout.

He picked up the camera draped around his neck and took a couple of shots before her eyes widened with surprise. "Don't worry. Not for publication. That look was too good to pass up, though."

"I'll get copies?"

"I'll make sure of it."

Her pout was gone as she glided away toward a small gathering of models. No doubt, she'd find someone else to go clubbing with her.

But, seriously. What was wrong with him? When had he ever turned a woman down?

Felicity's words rang in his ears. *You never stick around. As soon as you get what you want, you move on.*

He'd never thought of it like that. He had rules.

He never went out with the same woman more than twice, and he avoided compromising situations.

What was wrong with that? His mom would be proud, wouldn't she? He'd kept his honor while respecting the women he'd dated. They didn't want anything serious from him. When a model asked him out, it just meant she wanted a bit of eye candy on her arm. Not that she was suffering from unrequited love. At least not for him. His eye-candy presence had been used to make a wayward boyfriend jealous a time or two, to help catch an agent's eye, too. He didn't mind being used to advance a career all that much, but he wasn't a fan of being shoved into the middle of a relationship tussle. He'd learned that lesson the hard way. Now he went out of his way to avoid those particular types of situations. He preferred an uncomplicated life.

Hence the dating rules.

The models didn't seem to mind, either. Neither did the occasional actress or singer that he went out with. And, yeah, he asked them as often as they asked him.

But still.

There wasn't anything wrong with that.

Felicity obviously didn't know him. If she did, she wouldn't have said those things.

Which meant she wasn't the kind of woman he wanted to date. She had complication written all over her. In neon-bright permanent marker.

Nope.

Not interested in Felicity anymore.

So why had he said no to Marli/Karli?

If he wasn't bothered by what Felicity had said, why had he said no to what's-her-name?

CHAPTER FOUR

FELICITY PICKED UP HER GREEN-TINTED concealer.

One of the models had been sent for a touch-up, and if looks could be trusted, she had a cold. The green concealer was the best way to deal with the redness developing around the model's nose.

The woman threw herself into the makeup chair and rolled her eyes. "Do your worst."

Felicity went to work.

Some people liked to chat. Others didn't. Besides, it was the last day of the shoot. They'd been in Dresden almost a week and had worked all day, every day. Everyone was tired. Felicity knew better than to take it personally when someone sat quietly in her chair.

The model immediately started talking to another model in their little dressing room.

Hm. Maybe it was personal after all.

When she'd taken the job as a makeup artist, Felicity's mom had questioned her about the wisdom of her choice.

She had tried so hard to be tactful that she'd never gotten around to asking any questions.

Models are all so slender.

Sometimes when a woman is around beautiful women, she can start to feel...

I would hate for you to doubt yourself...

Envy is never a good thing, dear.

Mom had been right. Felicity had battled envy, jealousy, insecurity, and more since she'd taken the job. She was a normal-sized woman who spent her days surrounded by women any sensible doctor would label underweight.

Plus, she was a makeup artist. She was the help. And the help was ignored way more than it was recognized.

She'd never felt invisible until this job.

Every time she got fed up and started to type her letter of resignation, God stilled her hands.

You are my beloved child.

Five years on the job, and while she'd learned a lot about makeup, she'd learned even more about God. About herself, too. Not to mention who she was in Him.

Somewhere along the way, God had started showing her how important it was to love the people He put into her path. It was a call to unconditionality. She didn't get to love only the people who treated her well or those who thanked her for the work she did. God had called her to love every single person He placed in her path.

Some days were easier than others.

"Can't believe he said no."

"...always such a gentleman."

"...not often a man escorts me around town and doesn't expect anything in return at the end of the date..."

The models were chatting about someone. But who? They

didn't usually date the same man.

Except for…

"Piero the Playboy," Patrice whispered in her ear. "He turned Marli down when she asked him out. Been turning everyone down since you two did the tango on a sliding rug."

Felicity snorted. "Don't look at me. If he turned Marli down, he must have already had his evening's entertainment lined up."

Patrice gave Felicity's shoulder a light squeeze. "You have my permission to eavesdrop."

Then the model slipped past Felicity and joined the conversation. "I went out with Piero in Milan once."

"Milan?" One of the models sighed dreamily. "I went out with him in New York. I wish I'd waited till Milan to ask him."

Felicity reached for primer.

"Maybe he finally found a woman who makes him want to settle down."

"Or he's finally ready to come out of the closet."

Her hand stalled out en route. Gay? Piero?

"Face it. He never goes past the door when returning a woman to her room."

"And he only kisses on the cheek."

"Definitely gay."

"Seriously. Who could turn down all of this?" The model who'd made the closet comment ran her hands up and down her sides. Because she was just that hot. Obviously no straight man would ever say no to her.

Felicity shook her head and swallowed a more-sarcastic-than-sincere comment as she started applying primer around the now-concealed red nose.

He hadn't *felt* gay. Not that she'd know what a gay man felt like. Or a straight one for that matter. After she'd climbed off of him that first day of the shoot, she'd gone running for the safety of the dressing room not because she's been offended. Rather, the electricity lighting up every nerve-ending in her body had sent her scrambling. Or it had scrambled her brains. She still wasn't sure which.

"Watch it." The red-nosed model snapped the words at her.

Felicity blinked and looked at what she was doing. Her hands here shaking. Actually shaking. And shaking hands did not apply even makeup. "Sorry."

Once the primer was finished, she reached for the foundation. The other models had wandered off. Maybe she could ask... "I always thought Piero slept around. Piero the Playboy. He had to get that name from somewhere."

The model rolled her eyes without twitching so much as even a single facial muscle. "Playboy because he only plays at dating. Never goes out with the same woman more than twice, and never goes past the front door when the night's over."

"Oh." Felicity moved on to the various powders needed to create an even finish the camera would love. She'd been on the same shoots as Piero before. How had she never heard this?

"But don't worry. He'd never bother with someone like you. I'm sure our playboy will stay far, far away from you and your front door."

Felicity's eyes snapped up to meet those of the model.

Malice poured from the woman's eyes.

Ah. So not one of the models who would ignore her.

And not kind, like Patrice.

Felicity offered a tight smile. "No worries there. My front door's not open for business anyway."

CHAPTER FIVE

PIERO STRETCHED HIS ARMS WIDE and lifted his face to the Italian sunshine.

There was something about Rome.

He loved Nonna's villa and the fond memories it held. Tuscany would always be *nel suo cuore*. It would always be in his heart.

But Rome…

Rome thrived with energy and an eclectic kind of excitement that got inside his blood and made him want to soak in the beauty of its mood.

His brother Nick laughed at him whenever he talked about cities as though they were living things. It was true, though. Every city he'd ever been in held a different personality. From the color of the sky, to the sound of the people, to the taste of the air — each was unique.

And Rome was one of his favorites.

He jumped at the chance anytime an opportunity to do a photo shoot in Rome came up.

Piero dropped his arms to his side, smiled at the older couple walking past him arm-in-arm, and took off at a light jog toward Trevi Fountain, the site of that day's shoot.

He beat half the models to the covered tent that housed a small dressing room and held his gear for the day.

The whispers stopped as soon as he stepped through the tent's arched entrance.

He should be used to it by now. Whispers had been following him all week.

That's what happened when a man who was apparently known for his dating practices suddenly stopped dating.

People talked.

Some with curiosity.

Some with jealousy.

It was the nature of the industry. If he couldn't handle it, he'd have left it years ago.

"*Buongiorno*," he called out in a general greeting to everyone in the tent. "Are we ready to get started today?"

Lizbeth, the hyper-energetic former cheerleader in charge of coordinating the models bounced on her toes. "You're early. We're still waiting for three."

Piero tossed her a careless shrug. "It's a beautiful day. No reason to stay holed up in a hotel when I could get out and enjoy the sun. Can we get started with the ones we have, or are the other three in every shot?"

She blinked her big, blue eyes at him before looking down at her clipboard. When she looked back up, she nodded. "Of course we can go ahead."

Then she nodded again, as if trying to convince herself.

Lizbeth then stuck two fingers in her mouth and let out a shrill whistle before calling the names of the models who would be in the first shots.

Piero shook his head and reached for the camera he wanted. He picked up a second camera and draped it around his neck. Better to be over prepared than under…

They were doing a shoot for a winter edition, so the models traipsed out of the tent in their short dresses, thigh-high boots, and fur coats. Magazines had to plan far in advance. He almost always ended up shooting Christmas scenes in July and swim suit models in December, but that was just the way things went.

"Be sure to stay hydrated, ladies. We can't stop every five minutes, but if somebody needs a break to cool down, speak up." He unscrewed the lens cap and checked the lighting through his viewfinder before snapping some test shots as the assistants worked to arrange the coats and the models wearing them.

"That's a wrap!" Lizbeth's too-cheerful voice carried across the crowd gathered in front of the fountain.

Between critiquing the makeup, the positioning of the models, and Piero's choice of lighting techniques, she'd more or less taken over the entire shoot.

The power had gone to her head. Either that, or she needed a good, solid lesson in professionalism. Maybe he could put in a word and get her assigned to a shoot with Charise. She'd either be receptive to learning or not. He couldn't control that, but he could make an effort not to write her off after just one time working with her.

Even if he really, really wanted to.

On the bright side, they weren't going to cross paths again anytime soon. She wasn't working any of the shoots he was assigned to in the next three months.

Thank goodness for small favors.

Or big ones.

This might qualify as a big one.

"Piero! *Caro cugino!*" Alessa gave him a wide wave as she wove through the now-dispersing group of people.

"Cousin, look at you." He let out a whistle before pulling her into a hug and giving her the traditional European greeting of a kiss on each cheek. "I keep telling you — you should be on the cover of a magazine."

She pushed him away. "*Stupido.*"

He clutched his chest. "So cruel! Like a knife to my heart."

Alessa offered him an exaggerated eye roll. Apparently Felicity wasn't the only woman immune to his charms.

Piero laughed. "So where are you taking me?"

"You sure you don't mind?" She tipped her head toward their transportation.

"Riding on the back of a scooter while a beautiful woman drives? You must not know me as well as I thought."

Alessa shook her head, her auburn hair catching flight in the breeze. "Are you ready?"

He hooked a thumb toward the small tent. "Let me get my gear packed up. The agency is sending it on to France for me, but I like to…"

"Go. Make sure all your babies are properly packed away in their padded cages."

Piero made quick work of storing his bulkiest cameras in their dry boxes and signing the paperwork that handed possession of them over to the agency's representative. Then he paid the waiting courier to deliver the remaining cameras back to his hotel. They'd be there waiting for him when he returned from dinner with Alessa.

"Alright, *mi bella dama.* Lead the way."

"Fair lady? What? Are we living in the 1950s now?" Alessa led him toward the white scooter she'd left on the side of the street.

"You never did answer. Where are we going?"

"Dinner on the piazza. There's a great little café. They'll be offended if we stay less than two hours."

"That's one of the things I love about Italy. Dinner takes hours and conversations take days."

Alessa strapped on the helmet she'd been carrying before slipping off her backpack. She pulled a second helmet from the dark recesses of the pack and tossed it to Piero. Then she returned the now-featherweight pack to its usual place on her back and climbed onto her scooter.

He buckled his helmet — she had to have given him pink on purpose — before settling onto the seat behind her. "Alright, cuz. Let's do this."

Alessa started the scooter then pulled away from the curb as twilight descended on the city of Rome.

Oh, yeah. There was something about the smell of the air in Rome. Especially with the moon rising and the company of family.

An hour later, they came to a stop in the shadows around the corner from the Piazza Santa Maria in Trastevere. Piero hopped off the scooter and removed his helmet. "I always get my hotel close to the shoot site. I forgot what it's like to drive in Rome."

"Tonight was a tame night. I only used my horn a dozen times." Alessa shoved the pink helmet into the backpack and threaded the strap of hers through the backpack's shoulder hole so she could secure it into place.

Before she could pull the backpack onto her back, though, Piero grabbed it from her and slung it over his shoulder. "You ever going to get that thing for the back of your scooter so you don't have to lug your helmet with you everywhere you go?"

Her smile wasn't the least bit sheepish. "Every time I think about it, I see a new pair of shoes I can't live without."

Piero hooked his arm with his cousin's. "Now why doesn't that surprise me?"

She led the way to a café at the edge of the piazza. "Our fountain here is the oldest fountain in Rome. It dates back to the eighth century."

He laughed at her change of subject. "Don't worry. I won't tell the cousins what a maniac you are on that scooter. Or about your shoe addiction."

Ninety minutes later, a waiter slid two gelatos onto their table and refreshed their coffee.

Piero stared out over the piazza.

Alessa nudged his foot with her own. "Who is she?"

"Hm?"

"At least five different women have tried flirting with you tonight. Maybe more. I wasn't paying attention at first."

"Oh?"

"And you didn't notice any of them. What gives? Either you've met someone, you've had a lobotomy, or you're not really my cousin Piero."

"Five? Really?"

She upped her game from a nudge to a light kick. "What gives?"

He rubbed the back of his neck. "I tripped a couple weeks back as I was walking onto a shoot. I landed on a rug and took a woman down with me. We skidded across the floor."

Alessa covered her mouth.

"Laugh all you want. I… She caught my interest. And I wanted to apologize."

"Classic Piero. Let me guess. A ginormous bouquet and the best local chocolate you could find."

Heat clawed its way up his neck. "I asked her out to dinner the next day."

"And she turned you down?"

"Flat. Told me I went out with a different woman every day and she wanted nothing to do with me or my reputation."

"Hm."

"It's not as bad as all that."

Alessa pushed her empty bowl to the side. "I almost unfollowed you on social media because all your lady loves keep taking selfies with you and tagging you in them. My newsfeed was so full of your face that I missed it when one of my friends' nonna had a stroke."

He winced. "I'm not *doing* anything. I just don't see the point in hanging out alone in a hotel room night after night."

"I get it. A little. Maybe. But rug-lady has a point."

He choked.

"Hey, if you don't give me her name…"

"And have you splash it all over social media? Not in a million years."

"Rug-lady it is then."

He shook his head. "Come on, cousin. I have an early flight, and you're my ride back to the hotel."

She jumped up from her seat, circled the table, and snapped a selfie of the two of them before Piero could protest. She tossed him a wink. "Don't worry. I'll tag you in it."

Alessa dropped him off at the hotel's entrance with a hug, and Piero made his way inside. As soon as the elevator doors closed behind him, his phone started buzzing.

A text from his older brother Marco. *So who's the girl?*

And a text from his twin brother Nick. *When were you going to tell me you met someone?*

Apparently Alessa didn't keep secrets very well. Then again, he hadn't asked her to.

Had he really met someone? He'd been prepared to write Felicity off. The one that got away.

Then he'd looked at his schedule for the next three months to make sure he wasn't going to run into Lizbeth again anytime soon. And he'd seen the details for his next shoot.

Makeup artist: Felicity von Wolff

His heart had done funny things, the sorts of things he wasn't used to.

Maybe Alessa wasn't as far off the mark as he wanted her to be.

He'd been a fool to think he could walk away from Felicity without a fight.

CHAPTER SIX

THE END OF MAY WAS closing in as Felicity stopped at a sidewalk café along the edge of *Place des Vosges*, Paris' oldest planned square.

A waitress approached. "*Vous désirez?*"

Felicity didn't visit France often enough to learn the language, but she'd picked up enough cues to know it was time to order. "*Café crème, s'il vous plaît*. And a croissant."

The waitress flashed a smile before disappearing back into the café. At least it hadn't been a pained smile. Felicity's accent was awful, but she'd learned enough to be able to order coffee, ask where the bathroom was, and say please and thank you. And croissant… Well, that was a French word to start with. Hard to go wrong there.

When the waitress returned with her mocha latte and pastry, Felicity nodded to her. "*Merci.*"

"*Je vous en prie.*" Not *you're welcome*, but something close.

Felicity could ask her phone to translate, but something about people watching in Paris made technology seem superfluous.

Instead, she turned her chair to the square and settled in for a spell.

What better way to shake off the stress of travel than to enjoy a good mid-morning coffee in an open-air café?

A last-minute change at her previous shoot in Cleveland, Ohio, had put her into Paris a day earlier than planned. Not that she was complaining. She'd arrived late the night before. Thank goodness the hotel had been able to accommodate her. She might have ended up sleeping in one of the city's squares otherwise.

An extra day in Paris with no one telling her what to do?

Bliss.

Dusk fell over the city as Felicity made her way back to the hotel, a six story townhome-style building sandwiched between a law office and a beauty salon in Paris' historic Saint Georges district.

Nighttime in Paris was full of noise. People talking and laughing, the constant hum of traffic, and the occasional dog barking as though its life depended on its volume.

Paris wasn't romantic in the way Americans typically thought of it, but it had a romance all its own. Paris was a city of interconnected individuals who loved life and made no excuses for living it to its fullest. The people were passionate about taking even the most ordinary moments and making them extraordinary.

"Mademoiselle von Wolff!"

Felicity's head snapped toward the hotel's reception desk. The young man in the navy and black uniform came around the counter as her gaze landed on him.

"Mademoiselle von Wolff, a package arrived for you." He carried a cardboard tube with white plastic caps at both ends.

She took the tube and weighed it in her hand. It was too short to hold a poster. It weighed more than a poster, though. Not that anyone would be sending her a poster in Paris anyway.

For that matter, who would send her *anything* in Paris?

She slipped a five euro note to the eager young man and continued on to the grand staircase that would take her up to the second floor. From there, she boarded the elevator and rode it the rest of the way to the sixth floor before disembarking and digging out her room's key card.

Once inside, she closed the door behind her, set her small travel wallet on the dresser, and removed the tape from one end of the tube. She pulled the cap off and peered inside.

Say what?

She tipped the tube over to dump out its contents. A white business card tumbled out and came to rest on the bed's coverlet.

She looked inside the tube again before picking up the card.

The card had a rich texture and was made of heavy-weight, white stock with an embossed rectangle setting it off from the rest of the card. Inside that inner rectangle, two words were scrawled in the kind of elegant script she'd never been able to master.

Identity Mistaken

What did that even mean?

She flipped the card over. Nothing on the back.

Weird.

She set the card back down and reached her fingers inside the tube to pull out the remaining item.

Once she withdrew it, she laid it on her bed.

A canvas.

Oil painting, by the look of it.

A portrait.

And it looked just like…

No.

That didn't make sense.

But still.

Piero?

Not really. It didn't have Piero's face. The eyes, though. Something about those eyes immediately reminded her of Piero.

Or... One eye. Could a portrait have two faces on it?

The painting's background depicted a hillside vineyard filled with lush greens and purples off in the distance. Reminiscent of some Renaissance paintings. Saliba came to mind. As did some of Dosso Dossi's tamer works. Da Vinci, too.

The portrait in the foreground, though, was reasonably contemporary. A man in a charcoal pinstriped suit. The lapels were a little too wide to be current. The 70s? Maybe the 80s.

Black hair, ebony eyes. There were subtle differences, though. The cheekbone on the right side of the face was slightly higher and narrower than on the left. The right eye was a tiny bit wider than the left.

The painting pulled Felicity in. She didn't want to look away. But why? What was it about this odd portrait? It couldn't just be that first glimpse of recognition. She didn't even like the insufferable lout, so if anything, being reminded of Piero should make her dislike the painting.

She closed her eyes and turned away from where the canvas laid spread out on her bed. The image wouldn't leave her, though.

She opened her eyes and reached for the canvas.

Time to get answers.

CHAPTER SEVEN

PIERO TUGGED ON HIS HOTEL door to make sure it had latched behind him.

He didn't have any plans, but the quiet of the room was getting on his last nerve.

A quick turn to his left headed him in the direction of the elevator. And a familiar face. "Pardon me, Felicity."

Her eyes widened, and her grip tightened on the rolled canvas in her hand. "Piero?"

She looked like she'd seen a ghost. Surely she didn't despise him quite that much? "Aye."

Her gaze flicked from him to the canvas and back again. "You're working this shoot?"

"Unless I've been fired and no one told me." His quip got no returning smile.

"I, uh…"

Piero could stand there in the hallway all evening and remain perfectly content. Felicity, on the other hand, looked like she'd rather be anywhere else. His flagging ego took another hit. Giving up wasn't in his nature, though. Especially when he wanted something. And he wanted Felicity to like him. He wanted her to see that there was more to him than his reputation.

He took a half-step toward her and reached for the canvas. "What do you have there?"

She loosened her grip, and he pulled it from her hand. He unrolled the canvas and held it out in front of him.

And took a punch to the gut. "I know this face."

Felicity leaned in. "I thought he looked like you when I first saw him. It's not you. I could see that almost immediately, but something about the eyes…"

It made her think of him, huh? Maybe there was hope after all.

Piero tilted his head to the left. "The lighting is all wrong."

"Hm?"

"Portrait work is a lot like photography. You want the lighting to flatter and highlight the subject. The man here is cast in shadow, though. It makes his features indistinct."

"In a way that makes you think you can't quite trust what you're seeing."

He nodded his approval. "Exactly."

"When I look at it from one angle, I see sadness. But from another angle…"

"Fear." Piero finished for her.

"Fear… That's it. I couldn't quite figure it out before. I was too caught up in the difference between the two sides."

"But blended perfectly."

"Right? Would someone who doesn't work with people's faces for a living even see a difference?"

"Maybe. Maybe not." He wanted to study the painting, not roll it back up. It wasn't his, though, and he needed to relinquish it. What Felicity thought of him was more important than what he thought of the painting. And he needed to change the impression she had that he was a man who took what he wanted when he wanted. She hadn't said that before, but it had been there in the subtext of her accusations.

So he rolled the painting up and handed it back to her. Even though his hand fought his command to release it into her care. "Where did you get it? I'd be interested in asking the artist what he sought to accomplish."

Her shoulder lifted. "It was waiting at the front desk for me when I returned this evening. I was just going down there to ask about it."

"A canvas? At the front desk?"

Color stained her ivory cheeks. "It was in a cardboard tube, but the only direction on the tube was my room number. No information about the sender."

"Can I see it?"

Her gaze slid away from his. What was going on in that head of hers?

"I, uh... Sure. Hold on." She slipped a keycard from her pocket and turned to the door on her right.

Once she had it open, she held the door for him. And that's when her reluctance clicked into place. His reputation. And that door opened into her bedroom. A temporary one, but still a bedroom.

She didn't know him, though. Not really, anyway. He didn't enter women's hotel rooms. It was a rule, and he kept it this time by leaning against the door, pinning it open with his body, as he waited for her to retrieve whatever she needed.

Felicity picked up a couple items off her bed and turned to the door. Her eyes flared wide for the barest hint of a second before she looked away.

Surprise. Fear. Desire. The widening of her eyes could convey any of those. If it had lasted even a second longer, he might have been able to identify which emotion was behind the action. As it was, he was left guessing.

She slid past him and into the hallway, keeping a three-inch wall of space between them the entire time. "Here. It came in this tube, and the only other thing in it was this card."

He took the delivery tube she held out. It had no identifying marks except for a single white sticker with a couple of typed words on it — the name of the hotel on the first line and *numéro de chambrer* with the number of her room on the second line.

Piero removed the end cap and peeked inside. Nothing. He reached for the card and turned it over in his hand.

Identity Mistaken.

That was it. Nothing else. No phone number. No website. Not even a watermark.

Nothing.

Hm. "You mind if I accompany you to the front desk? Paintings seem to have become a bit of a mystery in my family of late, and I find that yours is no less intriguing."

First Nonna, then Ric. Now... This might not be a mystery Piero could ignore for much longer.

CHAPTER EIGHT

"I'M SORRY, MA'AM. I HAVE no information about your package. It was already here when I came in this morning. The night manager will be in shortly, though. He may know more."

"Oh." Talk about anticlimactic. Felicity hadn't prepared herself for disappointment. She'd expected immediate answers.

Piero took her elbow. "Mademoiselle von Wolff will be in the café. Please send the night manager over when he arrives."

"Of course, monsieur."

Felicity allowed Piero to lead her to the hotel's café, but only because she wanted to go. It had nothing to do with the electric shock of his touch or the way it robbed her of the ability to speak. Or protest. Or run as fast and far as she could, which would have been the sensible approach to the situation.

Piero removed his hand from her elbow and pulled a chair out for her. Their table was at the edge of the café, almost spilling over into the hotel's lobby.

Her words caught up with her as she sank into the comfortable seat. "He said 'shortly.' What do you suppose that means?"

He waved a waitress over as he took his seat. "This is France. It could mean five minutes or five hours."

She chuckled. "I'm not sure I'm willing to wait five hours. We have an early shoot tomorrow."

Piero flicked his wrist. The overhead light reflected off the face of his watch. "I'm willing to give him two hours. If he's not here by then, I'll need to call it a night."

Felicity pulled her phone free from her pocket and swiped across its face so she could see the time. "I'd say ninety minutes, but let's play it by ear."

The waitress approached their table, a warm greeting on her lips.

Piero lifted an eyebrow in Felicity's direction.

She glanced at the chalkboard menu posted at the entrance. It all looked tempting, but… "I already had dinner."

Her companion rattled off something in French, too many words for her to follow, and the waitress walked off with a nod.

"So tell me about yourself. What led you to a career as a makeup artist?"

Felicity bit her bottom lip. It was hard to explain. "I kept changing majors in college. I thought I wanted to study art. Then photography. Followed by business management. Then one summer I got a job working as a gopher for a makeup artist on a movie set in my hometown. Something about it clicked for me. I changed my major and got a degree in special effects makeup."

His eyebrows drew together. "How did I not know that was an actual major?"

Something about his expression made her laugh. "Well, in your defense, it's usually found at schools that have strong theater departments and acting curriculums."

He snapped his fingers. "That's where I went wrong. I studied

50

photography at a private school in Baltimore. All they cared about was art, art, art. Nothing fun like theater."

"Ha. After I changed my major for the umpteenth time, I went to a university in the Shenandoah Valley. They pretended to offer lots of majors, but everyone knew they specialized in acting and dance." They were so different. He craved attention as much as she wished to avoid it. Would he understand if she told him that one of the things she liked the most about being a makeup artist was that she was almost wholly invisible?

No. He wouldn't understand. And even if he did, she wasn't ready to reveal that much about herself. She might be starting to believe that there was more to Piero the Playboy than she'd first thought, but that didn't mean she needed to open herself up and be — shudder — vulnerable with him.

Felicity took charge of the conversation. "You mentioned paintings and your family. Tell me about it. Do you have a painter in the family?"

He blinked. Maybe he didn't want the subject to change. Or he didn't like the subject she'd chosen. Regardless, he didn't argue. "It all started at Nonna's birthday party."

The waitress approached with a small tray. By the time she walked away, they each had an empty plate and glass of sparkling water, and their table was filled with delicate cucumber and gouda sandwiches, sliced bread accompanied by a variety of cheeses, miniature chocolate croissants, and a selection of colorful macarons.

Felicity blinked. "How did she fit all this on that tiny little tray?"

Piero's grin lit up his face. "This is Paris. Anything's possible."

She shook her head and found herself filling her plate with a sampling of everything. "So much for being full."

He winked. "I can skip a meal at home, no problem. Drop me

anywhere in Europe, though, and I'll find a way to fit extra meals into every single day just so I can enjoy the pleasure of the food."

Felicity needed to rein him in before they got entirely too far off-track. "So…Nonna?"

CHAPTER NINE

"MY GRANDMOTHER. HER EIGHTIETH BIRTHDAY was in April, and she called all the grandchildren to her Tuscan villa for a big celebration."

Felicity reached for another of the miniature cucumber and gouda sandwiches. "What does your grandmother's birthday have to do with my painting?"

Piero studied her across the table. *My painting.* Interesting. "Someone had sent her a painting, and nobody knew where it had come from. All us cousins were fascinated and decided we need to unravel the great painting mystery."

"Your liberal use of air quotes tells me you're not all that interested in the mystery?"

He shrugged. "Not at first. Then my cousin Ric got a painting, also anonymous."

Felicity had rested the cardboard tube on the third chair at their table. Every now and then, she reached over and tugged that chair a tiny bit closer. It appeared to be an unconscious motion, which made it all the more intriguing. "I'm not sure that explains your interest in my painting."

He lifted an eyebrow. "Did anybody ever tell you that you're too clever by far?"

"Only my grandmother, but I'm not sure she meant it as a compliment."

"Nonna's painting was framed, but Ric's arrived unmounted and rolled up in a cardboard tube with an embossed card."

Felicity's eyes widened. "You think this painting was intended for you?"

He crossed his arms and leaned back in his seat. "Maybe. Probably. But it was delivered to you."

She frowned. "It was delivered to my room. My name's not on it. What about Ric's tube? Did it have his name?"

"As far as I know, but I'm not sure I ever thought to ask. I might have just assumed it. He would have mentioned it if it had shown up without a name or address."

"I'm not sure…" Her words stalled out before they could make their escape.

"Not sure of what?"

She blinked as color crawled its way up her neck. "I'm not sure I want to let it go. Something about the painting calls to me."

"I understand. I thought my cousins were all overreacting. But now that I've seen this one, I think I get it."

"Is this one different than the others?"

"Yes. No. The style looks the same, but one was a landscape scene, and the other was a painting of two people from behind. Neither was a portrait, not in the traditional sense."

"And you understand portraiture."

He would have had to explain to anyone else. Felicity, though, seemed to *get him* without even trying.

She gave a small nod in the direction of the painting. "If you were a nature photographer, maybe the landscape would have captured your interest. But you photograph people. That's where your interest lies."

"That's where I see beauty."

"In fashion?"

"Ah, now you're backpedaling. You said it yourself. I don't photograph clothes. It's the people I want to capture." He would give almost anything to capture her unique beauty. He'd snagged a few shots without her noticing, but that was different. If she ever opened herself willingly to the camera, her photos would be breathtaking.

"Yes, well. It may not be yours." She glanced away, and color again bloomed on her cheeks. Perhaps he'd been staring a bit too intently.

"Of course." Who was she fooling? The painting belonged to him. Everything from the way it was delivered to its resemblance to him — everything pointed to it being Piero's. The only question was how she'd ended up with it in the first place.

The night manager chose that moment to approach them. "Mademoiselle von Wolff. Monsieur Carter. I'm told you have a question about a delivery?"

Felicity lifted the cardboard tube from its perch. She clutched it to her chest for the barest hint of a second before handing it over to the night manager. "I wondered if you had any information on who delivered this."

He waved the tube away. "I double-checked the logbook to make sure I remembered correctly. It was delivered by courier late last night."

Piero sat up straighter. "Courier? Do you have the name of the courier service?"

"Unfortunately, no. It should have been recorded, but we happened to be especially busy when the courier brought it in. I signed for it myself but didn't double-check the courier service. I assumed there would be something on the package to tell me which service. There usually is, but not this time. It was odd."

Felicity bit her bottom lip before directing a question at the night manager. "Is there any chance this should have been delivered to Mr. Carter instead of to me?"

The man's brow furrowed. "This is your room number, is it not?"

She nodded.

"Give me a moment."

He bustled back to the front counter and began tapping away on one of the keyboards.

Felicity and Piero watched in silence from their little table.

The manager's face relaxed and Piero sucked in a breath. "I guess he figured it out."

A few hurried steps later, and the manager was once again at their table. "It appears, Mademoiselle von Wolff, that you arrived a day earlier than expected. Your room wasn't ready yet, so we put you into the room next to it — the one that had been reserved for Monsieur Carter here. When he arrived later, we put him into your previously assigned room."

Her face paled.

Hm. That pretty much explained it. The painting had been directed to him, not Felicity.

Piero swallowed.

Just how hard was it going to be to get that painting out of her hands?

CHAPTER TEN

"Oh." Eloquence wasn't Felicity's strong suit, at least not that evening.

Piero gave a small nod. "Well then. I guess that makes sense."

"Is there anything else?" The manager stood at attention.

"Not that I can think of. We'll let you know if there is."

The manager gave a slight bow before heading back in the direction of the front desk.

One of Piero's eyebrows lifted as his gaze again roamed over her, touching her face more intimately than a caress. Heat again climbed her neck and spread across her cheeks. Felicity tore her attention away from his eyes and stared over his right shoulder instead. "I... I guess this is yours then."

His eyes crinkled in the edge of her vision. "I suppose it is. How fortuitous, though, that it first made its way into your hands."

"Fortuitous?"

"We wouldn't have enjoyed this evening's chat otherwise. And I have. Enjoyed our chat, that is. Perhaps you have, too...?"

She studied his full lips for a moment before her gaze collided with his eyes. Piero may not be the playboy she'd first thought, but he was a dangerous man nonetheless, and she needed to be careful, lest she fall under his spell. "I… I think I recognize the painter."

Humor danced in his eyes, but he didn't speak. A slight nod, the only indication that she should continue.

"There's something about the brush strokes. I recognize it. And the use of shadow. I've seen this style before. I can't remember when or from where, but it's familiar."

"Hm. Think on it. If it comes to you, I'd love to hear anything you have to say. For that matter, even if it doesn't come to you…"

A laugh escaped Felicity before she could grab it back. Nerves. He made her uncomfortable. That had to be it. Because she surely wasn't giggling like a schoolgirl whose crush was talking to her for the first time. "I, uh, should probably turn in. Early morning and all that."

"Of course." Piero stood, tucked his chair in under the table, took the painting from where it rested, and held out his arm to her.

What was she supposed to do in the face of such gallant behavior? Was he being a gentleman? Or, under it all, was he the skilled womanizer she'd accused him of being? Her head and heart warred over the answer to that question.

Seeing no easy way out of it, Felicity slipped her arm through Piero's and allowed him to lead her up the grand staircase and to the elevator. He said not a word when the doors slid closed. Nor when they opened again on her floor — their floor.

He stopped in front of her door. As soon as she pulled her hand from his arm, he took a half step back. She was grateful for the distance. It was far too difficult to think clearly with him close.

Felicity fumbled with her key. She put it in backwards first then got it right on the second try. As she opened her door, she turned to wish Piero a good night.

He stood there, the painting tube clutched in one hand, an unreadable expression on his face. "I'll see you in the morning then."

She nodded. "Bright and early."

He glanced away and then back at her. "We could head out together in the morning if you'd like. Grab a croissant and coffee along the way."

Felicity blinked. What did she say to that? It almost sounded like a date. And… "If we show up at the shoot together…"

"It'll look like we ran into each other on our way there."

He could be right. Or not. But did it matter? As long as she knew she hadn't done anything wrong… She gave him a nod. "Very well. I'll meet you in the lobby in the morning. What time?"

"Half past five? That should give us plenty of time in case we run into trouble. Give me your cell number, though, to be on the safe side."

She pulled out her phone and hit the button so she could connect with his. Even as she sent her electronic contact card to his phone, she questioned the wisdom of the action. At a time when she should be fortifying her boundary walls, she was instead tearing them down.

"Your cameras are already there?" Felicity shook her head. Why couldn't she stop talking and send him on his way?

Piero's head tilted to the side, and his eyebrows drew together. "For the most part. I have a couple I'll carry with me in the morning, but most of them are on-site."

"Someday you'll have to tell me why you need so many."

A smile flashed across his face and brightened his chocolate eyes. "*Someday*. I like the sound of that."

CHAPTER ELEVEN

PIERO WATCHED THE DOOR CLOSE behind Felicity before he moved down the hallway to the next one and slid his key into the card reader.

Someday.

The word implied a future. She might not realize it, but Felicity had just given him a precious gift — hope.

It must be Paris. Something about leaving Felicity at her hotel door and knowing that only a thin wall separated their rooms was harder than he would have imagined. He'd never worked this hard to walk away from a date before, and he wasn't even sure their shared table at the café could be called a date. They'd been killing time while they waited for the night manager to show up.

Was that a date?

Piero pulled out his phone and tugged the painting from its tube. He laid it out on his bed, weighing the corners down with whatever was handy — a brush, a Bible, his wallet, and his watch. Then he took a couple of pictures with his phone and sent them via the family's group text.

This arrived but got delivered to the wrong person by accident. I'm dialing her in on the convo in case she has anything to add.

He added Felicity's number to their group.

It seemed like a great idea, too, until replies from his cousins started flying in.

Where are you? — Paris

Who got the painting? — A woman I work with

This one's darker than the last.

It's a portrait, too. With a single focus. That's new.

What do you think it means?

Has anyone talked to Nonna lately? Nobody's let this slip, right?

A private text came in then. *Um. Why am I getting all these texts?*

Uh-oh. He should have told Felicity what he was going to do. What if she was one of those people who never turned her phone off or put it on silent? This would be a long night for her. *My cousins. We have a group text. I added you to the group. Figured since the painting got delivered to you, you had a right to be a part of things.*

He waited for a reply, but when five minutes passed without one, he followed up with another text. *Should I not have?*

The reply came almost instantaneously. *I don't know. I was confused. See you in the morning.*

It could have been worse. She could have demanded he remove her from the group conversation. She could have told him he was on his own in the morning. She could have pounded on the wall they shared and yelled at him through it.

So he'd call this a win.

Someone should make that a hashtag.

#nottickingoffthewomanyoulikeforthewin

Piero took a couple more shots of the painting, this time with his camera. Then he rolled the canvas up and stored it in its tube.

Morning was going to arrive far too soon, and he needed to be at his best. His job demanded it, and the pretty makeup artist he'd be sharing breakfast with deserved it. So like a responsible adult, Piero got ready for bed, and climbed between the crisp, clean sheets.

And lay there.

And lay there.

And kept lying there.

Sleep apparently didn't want to visit him.

So Piero stared at the ceiling.

Had his life been incomplete? He'd spent the last several years keeping women at arm's length. He hadn't been immoral or promiscuous, but he also hadn't allowed himself to invest in people or in relationships.

He'd chosen a career that moved him from place to place and moved people though his life like water through a sieve. Until now, the only people he'd ever wanted to keep from falling away were his brothers and parents. His cousins, too, to a lesser extent.

And maybe that was the problem.

He picked up his phone again. Nicolò —Nick — would understand. Piero tapped out a message. *Sometimes I wonder if Mom's death hit me harder than I realized.*

Nick's reply was almost instantaneous. *Me too. Sometimes. In what way?*

How could he put it into words?

No, that wasn't the real question.

Was he brave enough to put it into words? Was he ready to stop hiding?

His heart twisted in his chest as he thought of Felicity sleeping on the other side of their shared wall. Did she have any idea how much introspection she'd caused in a man she considered shallow and incapable of deeper thought?

Relationships. Women. Would I have done things differently? You know?

A couple minutes later, the phone lit up with Nick's response. *God's grace covers a lot. Even pigheaded twin brothers who make up a dumb two-date rule to avoid commitment. Or to avoid letting anyone get close.*

Piero snorted. *Gee, thanks. And when will you be publishing your music?*

He added a winky emoticon at the end. Nick would get it. He would know his twin wasn't nagging. Nick's words, though, were probably more right than he realized.

Their mom's death had hit them all hard, but they were men. Strong, Italian-American men. They'd probably all buried their emotions and their hurt deeper than was good for any of them.

The thing was that Mom hadn't been perfect. She'd had her share of faults, but those faults had never made her less of a person. They'd made her more somehow. More real. More human. More lovable. And more loving.

Then she was gone, and she had become the missing piece of every puzzle in Piero's life, the missing part of every conversation.

The mysterious painting came to mind. Piero climbed out of bed. He didn't bother with the lights. He pulled the painting from its tube and held it up by the window. The glow from the city lit up the canvas just enough for him to study the two sides of the face. The differences were subtle, but there were definitely two distinct faces — or half of each of the two — and that had to mean something.

But what?

Piero was on the cusp of change. The path of his life was approaching a fork in the road, and he was going to need to decide who he wanted to be.

Had the man in the painting faced a similar decision? Had he worn a mask? Had he shown the world more than one face? Did he find it necessary to give one of them up at some point? Or did the painting mean he'd never decided between the two?

Piero, too, had more than one. Maybe it was high time he made a decision instead of drifting through life. Which face was he going to keep? And which was he going to put down?

Did he want to be Piero the Playboy? The man who never let anyone close and who avoided entanglements by keeping the world at arm's length?

Or did he want to be the sort of man that a woman like Felicity could confide in and laugh with? Did he want the pain and disappointment that came when you allowed your life to get tangled up with someone else's and then they left?

Piero put the painting away and reached for his clothes.

Maybe a walk would help him clear his head.

He hoped so.

Because he didn't want to be a zombie in the morning when he met Felicity.

Which sort of answered the whole question, didn't it?

He cared what Felicity thought of him.

He didn't want her to pass through the sieve.

CHAPTER TWELVE

FELICITY FUMBLED IN THE DARK room as she reached for her phone.

That blaring had to stop.

It couldn't be morning already.

Could it?

She typed in the code to silence her alarm.

Once upon a time, all she'd had to do was tap the screen to silence it. But it had become too easy for her to tap and fall back asleep. So she'd installed an app that made her type in a code to shut off her alarm. The theory was that it would force her brain to wake up enough to realize she really did need to get out of bed.

And it worked. Most days. Thankfully this was one of them.

Thirty minutes later, she was showered and dressed with her hair pulled back in the ponytail she normally wore to work.

She grabbed her satchel and the wheeled suitcase that held the tricks of her trade.

As the elevator began its descent to the second floor, she pulled her phone from her pocket. With her folks in America, she often got texts from them during the night. Time zones got too complicated, so she just told them to text or call whenever they wanted and not to have hurt feelings if they didn't hear back for several hours. That was easiest.

The elevator doors opened, and Felicity made her way to the stairs and down to the lobby and a comfortable-looking wingback chair. Piero should see her as soon as he started down the elevator.

A quick swipe of her finger brought up her phone's home screen.

With all its notifications.

Too many notifications.

One hundred and eighty-three notifications.

What on earth?

She tapped the button and saw a text from her mom and one from Aunt Gemma.

And one hundred and eighty-one from Piero's family.

Her lungs froze as though they'd forgotten how to breathe.

She scrolled to the top of the conversation and started reading through.

Good grief. How could people have so much to say about nothing?

They fired comments and responses back and forth to each other as though they were all sitting around a big, noisy table.

Only, Felicity had never had a big table. Or a noisy one. She was an only child. The only loud conversations at her table happened when Aunt Gemma visited and insisted on talking about politics.

A moment later, Piero strode across the lobby's carpet, his camera bag slung over his shoulder.

"Ready to get going?" Despite his ready smile, the poor man had circles under his eyes.

"You didn't sleep much, did you?"

He shrugged. "I needed to do some thinking, so I went for a walk."

"Alone?" Was he out of his mind? Nobody walked alone in Paris at night. Unless they wanted to invite trouble.

"Me and God. I figured we could take anybody who gave us trouble."

She shook her head. "God gave you a brain."

He threw his head back and laughed. "Indeed he did. Which is why I pretty much just circled the block that our hotel is on."

"That's not a very long walk."

He winked. "I didn't say how many times I circled it."

She shook her head. He was being flirty again, but it was different somehow.

Before long, Piero was holding the door for her at a small café. The place was tucked away where one of the inlets fed into the *Bassin de la Villette*, the oldest manmade lake in Paris.

He pointed out a table. "You watch our bags, and I'll go order. Want something specific, or do you trust me?"

"Protein. I want something with protein. Otherwise, I don't care."

He came back a couple of minutes later with two steaming cups of coffee. "They'll bring our breakfast in a second. And we can get to-go cups when we're ready to leave."

"You have a huge family." Felicity blurted it out.

"I do." He set their cups down.

"And they've known each other for ages."

Piero pulled out his chair and sat. "I… Uh… I've known them all my life."

Her voice quieted. "I think they tease each other, too, but it sounds so serious in text. I kept expecting someone to get mad."

He nodded.

That was it? A nod? As if his family was normal.

"Do you have any brothers or sisters?"

Felicity shook her head. "I'm an only child."

"Cousins?"

"Two. They live in Montana. Small town. Rainbow Falls."

He nodded again. As if her family was normal, too. They couldn't both be normal, though. Could they?

Piero took a drink. "When's the last time you saw your cousins?"

How long had it been? "Five years. Maybe six. We had a family reunion."

"Are you close to them?"

"Well, sure. We talk on social media and stuff. Exchange Christmas cards. Talk on the phone now and then."

"How about when you get together? Do you have a lot to say then?"

She shrugged. "We used to. They have kids now, though, so I'm not sure. I'm not that interested in potty training or ordinal numbers. I mean…" Her voice dropped even lower. "…who sings a song just because someone went poo in a toilet?"

He threw his head back and laughed. "None of my cousins are married yet, let alone having kids. So I don't know. But I have a feeling that's part of life when you start a family. It could be worse, right? At least it's not a song *and* a dance."

Piero, Piero, Piero. Here she was being serious, and he had to go and make her laugh.

Her mom would tell her that's the kind of man she needed. That she took life too seriously. That she didn't laugh enough.

She didn't want to *need* a man, though. She wanted to choose one. And, nice as he was turning out to be, Piero wasn't the sort of man she would ever choose.

The waitress arrived with their order, and Felicity breathed in

70

the fragrant steam. Eggs Benedict was about as far from a traditional French breakfast as a person could get. She would savor every bite.

Piero lifted his fork, then paused and set it back down. "Do you mind if I bless the meal?"

She blinked. Piero the Playboy did not pray. But this Piero had cousins, a nonna, and a quiet strength to him. He went for long walks with God, too. Somehow it seemed perfectly good and right that he pray. "Sure. Go ahead."

He bowed his head. "Lord, thank you for this meal and the beautiful day in which to enjoy it. Please be with the shoot today and help things to go according to Your will. Be with Nonna and the cousins and with my brothers. And thank you. Of all the places that painting could have gone, it ended up in Felicity's hands. I thank you for that. Amen."

Felicity snapped her jaw closed as Piero looked up at her. She hadn't managed to close her eyes. Or bow her head. She'd been too busy being stunned at the words coming out of his mouth. Why had she always thought Piero was selfish and self-centered? In all the shoots they'd worked together, had she never actually bothered to have a conversation with the man? And she had thought *him* stuck up?

"What?" His eyebrow lifted. "I can't have food on my face. I haven't even started eating yet."

She shook her head more forcefully than necessary. "You're different than I thought."

"Given the opinion you so clearly expressed the day after our tumble in Dresden, I can only assume that the difference is an improvement…?"

She picked up her fork. He was teasing. He had to be. It was time she started to give him the benefit of the doubt. Maybe even tease him back. "Let's wait and see if we can get through today's shoot without me ending up flat on my back in front of the entire crew."

His brown eyes lit. "As I recall, I'm the one who ended up on my back. You, on the other hand, were comfortably sitting on top of me."

Heat flashed across her face. Leave it to him to remember that part. She was no good at this teasing thing.

"Don't worry. You'll get the hang of it."

Her gaze snapped to his. "Of what?"

The light in his eyes shifted, transformed somehow. The laughter was still there, but so was something else. What was it, though? "Of giving as good as you get. You just need practice, but you're a quick study. You'll be giving better than you get in no time. Then I'll be the one blushing and at a loss for words."

She dropped her gaze. She'd hoped the blush hadn't been one of her more noticeable ones, but no such luck.

Piero reached a hand across the table and brushed the back of her hand with his fingers. "Hey."

She looked up again.

"Don't let me and my wayward sense of humor rob you of knowing just how captivating you are."

This man... First laughter, then... Desire. That's what she saw in his eyes. It had to be. Because that was exactly what she felt.

But good Christian girls didn't give in to feelings like that.

She snapped off a nod before pulling her hand away from his, picking up her knife, and cutting through her breakfast.

She'd been attracted to men before, sure. She was only human, and she worked with models — not all of which were female. But desire?

She was in trouble.

Big trouble.

CHAPTER THIRTEEN

ASKING A WOMAN OUT AFTER a fourteen-hour workday wasn't ideal.

Felicity had kept distance between them ever since their breakfast the other day, though, and Piero wasn't ready to let her turn that pattern into a habit.

He waited until right before the last session when Felicity slipped out of the dressing room. Then he snuck in, grabbed her wheeled luggage-like makeup case, and rolled it over to the camera table. He tucked it behind two of his camera cases and hoped no one ratted him out before he was ready.

By the time Felicity walked back toward the changing room, Piero was clicking away with his camera.

Forty minutes later, the words rang out. "It's a wrap!"

All the models from that day's shoot were done. They would be flying out either that night on a redeye or early the next morning. A new group was coming in, though, for the next shoot in two days' time.

Which meant the shoot staff had an entire day off.

In Paris.

And Piero wasn't one to squander a chance like that.

"Hey there…" The voice dripped seduction.

"Uh, hi." Piero busied himself with his camera.

"Want to go out? I could show you…"

He glanced up in time to see her lick her lips.

"…a good time."

Felicity chose that moment to step out of the changing room, her brows drawn together.

Piero cast a glance at the woman whose name he couldn't remember. "No thanks. I have plans."

Her lips formed a careful pout. "That's too bad. You would have enjoyed yourself."

He moved toward the camera table. A couple months ago he might have… Piero shook his head. That woman had predatory written all over her. He wouldn't have gone out with her, even pre-Felicity.

Speaking of, he changed direction to intercept her. "Hey."

She blinked at him. "Uh. Hi. Have you seen my makeup case? It was in the changing room, but now it's gone."

"Maybe."

Her eyes narrowed.

"I, um, didn't want you to jet out as soon as the shoot was over, so I might have moved your case to delay you."

Her gaze flicked over his right shoulder before returning to his face. "Someone seems to want your attention."

Piero turned to where Felicity had been looking. The nameless model stood there, one hip thrust forward, her arms crossed and pushing up her barely covered attributes. Ignoring her, he returned his attention to Felicity. "Spend tomorrow with me."

"What?"

"Tomorrow. You. Me. Together."

Her gaze dropped as the *clickety-click* of high heels behind him announced the model's departure. "I'm not sure that's a good idea."

"It is."

She lifted her gaze to his.

"Trust me. It's a good idea."

"Why do you want to spend time with me?"

"You captivate me."

Her eyes flared wide.

"You don't dance around issues. You cut right to the heart of things. Even if that means slapping me in the face with my own reputation. And…"

"There's more? Because so far you've made me sound like a linebacker with PMS."

The laughter built in his chest, but he held it back. "You make me want to be a better version of myself. I don't know exactly what that means, but I know I'm not willing to let it go until I find out."

She bit her bottom lip. "Okay. Maybe not *quite* a linebacker."

He let the laughter out then. "Say you'll spend tomorrow with me. We can do anything you want, or I can plan the day."

She shrugged. "Okay, fine."

He bowed with a flourish. "Your enthusiasm overwhelms me."

She shook her head, but laughter danced in her eyes. "It's a good thing I'm fluent in snark. Otherwise, we might have a problem."

Piero waited in the lobby for Felicity to appear. He'd made a list of several things they might do in Paris. He generally liked to wing it.

He'd been known to get on a bus before and wait to see where the bus ended up before deciding what he was doing that day.

Felicity wasn't that kind of girl, though. She liked a little more control than that, and he didn't mind accommodating her in that regard.

Not that he'd share that bit of information with anybody in the family. He could still remember the time in high school that he'd had a crush on Vera Sanchez. As soon as his brothers had found out, they'd started following him around the house singing in falsetto. "Two little lovebirds sitting in a tree…"

Piero shook the reverie loose as soon as he saw Felicity at the top of the staircase. She wore black jeans, a midnight blue shirt covered in glittering starbursts, and she had an old-fashioned granny sweater in bright orange tied around her waist. She was the picture of perfection.

Felicity's smile was tentative. "Are we ready?"

He handed her a bag from the café. "A chocolate croissant. Enjoy it. I already ate mine, and it was the kind of fresh you can only get in France."

The caution in her eyes dissipated with her first bite. "Mm. Good."

Chocolate was always a winner. Wise words his dad had taught him years ago. "I wrote down some ideas of where we could go. Want to take a look?"

She nodded but didn't reach for the list. "Tell me."

"*Notre Dame*, the *Louvre*, *Musée d'Orsay* for anyone who's into impressionist or post-impressionist art, *Cimetière du Père Lachaise* — if you like old, famous cemeteries. Or there's *Marché aux Puces* — a famous flea market, *Basilique du Sacré-Cœur*, *Musée Rodin*, and *Musée des Égouts* because every woman who comes to Paris wants to visit the sewer museum. They also offer tours if a sewer museum isn't quite enough to whet your appetite.

What do you think?"

Laughter lit her eyes. "You came up with quite a list there. Are these all places you've been?"

Heat colored his cheeks. "Photo shoots, mostly. When I'm being a tourist, I like to visit the sites that don't generally make it into the books they sell tourists."

"I love Van Gogh, so *Musée d'Orsay* is a must." Mischief made her blue eyes sparkle. "And I've always wanted to tour the Paris sewers. I'm not sure you're dressed for it, though."

Piero followed her line of sight down to his shoes. "They're only shoes. What's a little sewer mud between friends, right?"

She swallowed the last bite of her chocolate croissant. "Indeed."

CHAPTER FOURTEEN

FELICTY NEARLY SQUEALED WHEN THEY stepped into the entrance of the *Musée d'Orsay.*

The museum was housed in an old train depot built more than a hundred years before. The architecture was breathtaking in and of itself, but the grand scale of everything made it more stunning than she'd been prepared for.

"Wow, wow, and wow."

Piero chuckled. "It's something else, isn't it?"

"Where do we start?"

"You said you like Van Gogh."

"We won't have time to see it all if we do more than glance."

"No reason to cram it all in on one visit. We can always come back another time."

She shot him a quick glance. *We?* One day of playing tourists didn't make them a *we.*

"Is it okay if we start and end with Van Gogh? I could spend the whole day just staring at his paintings, but I know there are other masters on display here."

By the time they made it through Van Gogh, Whistler, Caillebotte, Bazille, and Degas, they were both getting hungry. Felicity could have easily spent another hour soaking in Van Gogh, but Piero's stomach was getting louder.

He leaned in close. "People are starting to stare, and I'm afraid it's not at your beauty this time."

She swatted his arm. "So extravagant with the compliments."

"That doesn't make them untrue."

Maybe not, but they seemed false when they fell so easily from his lips. Perhaps that was her own insecurity at play. Better to change the subject. "Did you have something in mind for lunch?"

"Do you trust me?"

"That's a loaded question if ever there was one."

His muffled laugh tickled her ear. Meanwhile, his hand, barely touching her lower back, maneuvered them toward the exit as it sent shockwaves skittering up her spine. "I'm not sure whether to take that as a compliment or a challenge."

Felicity shook her head. The man was hopeless. Anything she said would just bait him.

As soon as they stepped out into the fresh air, Piero snagged Felicity's hand and tugged her along behind him. "If we walk, we can get to lunch in thirty minutes. If we try to get a ride, it'll be at least an hour."

She slipped her hand out of his grasp. "It's a good thing I like to walk. Where are we going?"

"It's a surprise…"

A half hour later, Piero paid for their tickets to the *Musée Rodin*.

"Lunch at a sculpture museum?"

"Come on." He reached for her hand again but stopped short of grabbing it. "Follow me."

In a few minutes, they were sitting down at a table. Did everybody know that a lovely little café was tucked away in the middle of the museum's sculpture garden? "Do you know where all of Paris' secret treasures are hidden?"

He gave a laughing shrug. "Not all of them. Just the good ones."

They took a brief tour of the garden, including Rodin's famous sculpture, *The Thinker*, while their meal was prepared.

"Depending on the subject, a sculpture can be a lot like a portrait." Piero waved a hand at a nearby sculpture.

"I've never thought of it like that, but I see your point. Sculptures have always kind of creeped me out."

"Ha. And I brought you into a garden of them for lunch."

"This place is lovely. Maybe I've just seen one too many shows where the sculptures turn out to be vicious man-eating monsters."

His eyebrows lifted. "What kind of shows do you watch?"

"The British kind. I'm a bit of a nerd when it comes to TV, I'm afraid."

"I knew there was a reason I liked you.

Their food arrived, and after a short blessing, Piero picked up the conversation again. "If you look at the sculptures, you can see that each is placed in the way that most flatters it."

Felicity glanced around the garden. She didn't have his eye for it, but she could sort of see how the light filtering down through the trees created different moods in the various nooks and crannies of the garden. "The lighting?"

He nodded. "Lighting, of course. But also the colors. The color of a dress worn by a woman is determined by her skin tone, right? She's not going to wear a color that doesn't flatter her. The sculptures are the same. They're placed around foliage that enhances their beauty, not dressed — as it were — with colors that hide their natural beauty."

Before long, they were pushing in their chairs and leaving the statue garden behind.

"How far to the sewer museum?" Felicity pulled out her phone and started tapping buttons to get to her map app.

He shrugged. "Twenty minute walk, maybe a little longer."

She stared at Piero. "You don't even need to map it, do you? Just how well do you know Paris?"

The barest hint of color climbed his neck. "I like to explore."

She shook her head. "All right. Lead the way."

"So what made you pick *Musée des Égouts*?" His voice carried a hint of mischief. "I can't think of many people who think touring the sewers of Paris is a great way to spend a day off in the city of romance."

She gave him a quick look, but his expression was inscrutable. Had he figured her out already? There wasn't really any point in lying about it. "I didn't want you to get the wrong idea."

"What would the wrong idea be?"

"That this is a date."

He finally met her gaze, and the laughter in his eyes was unmistakable. Somehow, though, he didn't seem to be laughing at her. "If it's not a date, what is it?"

"Two co-workers spending a day together, nothing more."

"Hm. Co-workers, huh? I don't know if co-workers tour the sewers together. There has to be at least some level of friendship there, wouldn't you say?"

Felicity's step faltered. She enjoyed his company, yes, but that didn't mean she was ready to think of him as a friend. "The jury's still out on that one."

Piero's laughter invaded Felicity's space. He wasn't a laugh-from-the-belly guy, but his laughter was no less inviting. Inviting enough that she found herself thinking of other ways to tease it out of him.

CHAPTER FIFTEEN

PIERO CHUCKLED AS FELICITY RACED past him and launched herself into the sunlight.

"Don't laugh at me!" Her admonition, called out between gasping breaths, was difficult to take seriously.

"You're the one who wanted to tour the sewers. What did you think it was going to smell like?"

"When I signed up for a tour of the Paris sewers —" Her breathing was almost back to normal. "— I thought we would be walking through historic sewers."

He couldn't help himself. She invited his jest the way a warm biscuit invited honey. "They were historic. Many of those sewers date all the way back to the 1850s."

"Historic." Felicity gave him a light shove. "As in, not actively in use."

Piero shook his head. "You could have asked. I'd have told you we'd be walking on platforms through the sewer tunnels."

"They have street signs, for pity's sake. Their sewer system has street signs."

He shook his head at her. "Because each sewer tunnel corresponds to the street above it. You need to know where you're at in those tunnels, or you could get lost down there."

"It was fascinating. Don't get me wrong. The next time we end up somewhere with a day to kill, though, if you're crazy enough to want to spend time with me, please stop me from choosing any other sewers or sewer-related sites to visit."

"You've seen one, you've seen them all?"

"I'm thinking so." She shuddered. "If not, I'm happy to live in ignorance."

The *Musée des Égouts* hadn't been that bad. Felicity had been completely engrossed in the tour guide's information, too. Until they'd hit a particularly odiferous passageway and her gag reflex had kicked in. Piero had never seen a woman turn green quite so quickly.

He was almost afraid to ask, but... "Is it too soon to mention that I made reservations for dinner?"

She gave him a glare. "Food? You're going to talk to me about food?"

"Come on. Trust me." He grasped her hand and tugged her along behind him... and she let him. Progress. He liked it.

They were practically on the bank of the Seine as it was. A short walk later, they were boarding a river cruise. The dinner service would open in an hour, and they had reservations in the boat's five-star floating restaurant. In the meantime, though, they could stay above and enjoy the fresh air.

"So, out of the blue? Just like that?"

Piero nodded. "I blinked, and suddenly I had a new cousin."

"That must have been hard for her."

He hadn't thought of it like that. "I was more focused on how it affected the cousins."

"But she's one of those cousins now."

A sigh slipped past his lips. "You're right, and I'm trying to treat her like one."

"By looping her in on a group text that's guaranteed to make her want to go hide her head in the sand?"

"That bad, huh?"

She gave him a half-shrug. "If going from being a land-loving creature to being dropped into the middle of the Atlantic and given only one inflatable arm band is bad, then yeah."

Piero took a drink of his sparkling water before setting the glass back down on the table. "Are we like that?"

"You've grown up with your family. Trust me. To an outsider, you all are an intimidating lot."

He rubbed his chin. "You might be right. I wonder if anybody has really tried to put themselves in Rachel's shoes."

"It's hard to imagine yourself in a stranger's shoes. Getting to know her ought to be the first step, but I can't imagine any of you really got to know her at your nonna's birthday party if the way you've described it is accurate."

Maybe. "She doesn't strike me as a wilting flower. She's a strong person. But your point is taken."

"I'm not trying to tell you what to do…"

"I know. And the insight's appreciated. I've reached out to her a couple of times, and I have plans to see her the next time I'm passing through that part of the world. I need to be more intentional about it, though. She doesn't say much, and we don't have the history for me to be able to read her silence. I was starting to think she didn't want this new family she'd been saddled with, but I need to rethink that."

Silence settled between them as they each finished their dinner. It was a contented silence, the kind of silence that follows good food, good conversation, and shared memories.

"I wish I'd brought my camera with me today."

"Photography wasn't allowed at any of the museums we visited. Except the…"

"Right? And I have brothers."

Felicity shook her head. "I'll never understand the male of the species."

Piero laughed. "Boys may grow into men, but they at least partially remain boys at heart. And if there's one thing I know about boys — from having been one, of course — it's that they love potty jokes and all things gross. I'll be retelling the Paris sewer story for a long time to come."

"Well, here we are." Felicity started to pull her keycard out but stalled out before she freed it from her pocket. "Indeed. Tomorrow's another early morning." Even so, he didn't want the evening to end.

"The shoot should be interesting." She made no move to open her door.

Piero nodded. "I saw the sketches. You'll have your work cut out for you."

"I'll get to use my airbrushes on this shoot."

"Ah, yes. I was on a shoot once where a model had an allergic reaction to the paint."

Felicity shrugged. "It's not common, but it happens sometimes. We're trained in what to do in case a model reacts."

A more gallant man would wish her a good night. "It should be a fun shoot. The designer wants his clothes to look fierce and sexy."

"Sure, but only a man would think dragons. Airbrush all the models so that they look like fierce dragons in disguise as sexy human women. It's going to be a blast, but still. Only a man would come up with that one."

Another couple passed by them in the hallway. It really was time to part ways and turn in. "I had a nice day."

Her blue eyes sparkled. "It's not often that I get to start the day with Van Gogh, eat lunch with a bunch of sculptures, visit a public sewer system, and then end the evening on the Seine River."

"Thanks—"

"Thanks—"

Piero grinned. "You first."

"Thank you for a lovely day. It was fun playing tourist with you."

"Come with me to meet Rachel."

Her jaw dropped, and her eyes widened. Uh-oh. Those were not *the* words he'd meant to say.

CHAPTER SIXTEEN

PIERO'S WORDS FILLED THE SPACE between them.

Come with me to meet Rachel.

"Uh…" What was Felicity supposed to say to that?

"Seriously. We might be heading in different directions first, but we're both going to end up in Scotland for the same shoot. I have a brief stopover in Cardiff. If you're flying the same route, you'll be stopping there as well. Rachel's going to meet me at the airport for lunch before I have to catch my next flight. Time your flight so you can come with me.

Meet his family?

"It might be nice for Rachel to meet someone who's not in the family, you know? Someone who understands how overwhelming we can be and who can sympathize with her."

It was a bad idea. Dumb, even.

Wasn't it?

They'd had a decent day together. A great day, even. She liked the parts of Piero she was getting to know. But…meet his long-lost cousin?

That was pure absurdity.

"Okay." Felicity clapped her hand over her mouth.

Piero gave her a bright smile. "I knew you'd see it my way."

She shook her head. "I didn't mean to say that."

"Of course you did. Haven't I already told you? You have a knack for speaking truth."

He leaned closer.

Felicity's heart jumped into the *tat-a-tat-tat* of a stampeding herd of wild mustangs. She wasn't ready for him to kiss her. They weren't there yet. She wasn't even sure she liked him like that. Sort of. But her hands refused to obey. Her fingers knotted together behind her back even as her brain shouted at them to pull the key card from her pocket.

Piero's warm lips brushed against her cheek. Then he spoke, his mouth near enough to her ear to send a wave of chills through her with each word. "I'll see you tomorrow."

He tugged the keycard from where it peeked out over the edge of her pocket, slipped it into the reader mechanism, and handed it back to her as he opened the door. "Enjoy your evening."

The door slid closed behind her, automatically locking.

Enjoy…?

What…?

On legs made of liquid goo, Felicity walked toward her bed. She collapsed onto the cover and rolled over until she lay on her back, looking up at the ceiling.

God, what are you doing here? I'm in trouble. Big trouble. He makes me feel crazy things I shouldn't be feeling. He's not the kind of guy I want to end up with. I like boring and stable.

She could almost hear God laughing at her. If she liked boring and stable, she wouldn't have chosen the career she had. She was a world traveling makeup artist. If she really liked boring and stable, she'd have become a family photographer and opened a nice little studio in a DC suburb near her parents.

The next two days flew by at supersonic speed. At one point, Felicity had been hanging, suspended from a cable, and lowered in above a model to touch up the makeup. The client had been very specific about the location of the models and hadn't taken into account the fact that once the moat filled and the shoot started, nobody would be able to get to them.

As precarious as the whole thing had looked, she'd been safe the entire time, and if she was being honest, those sorts of adventures were one of the reasons she loved her job. Physical adventures were like a well-crafted tiramisu — mouth-watering from the first bite to the last. The kinds of adventures that involved putting her heart at risk, though? Those too often had her reaching for the antacids.

Before she knew it, though, Felicity was packing her luggage and boarding a plane for New York. As one of the agency's traveling makeup artists, she was required to check in at headquarters about every six weeks. She spent a day or so filling out reports and another day or so talking to and helping to train new hires.

Traditionally, photographers, makeup artists, and the like worked for a single magazine or freelance. When the agency she worked through decided to put together a couple of groups of traveling photography teams, though, Felicity had jumped at the chance. She got to travel the world, and the agency, in turn, was able to provide a streamlined service to clients who wanted location-specific shoots.

She could make more money as a freelance makeup artist, but

Felicity liked the simplicity of working for an agency. They told her where to go and when, they took care of all the paperwork, and they handled the client and any problems that arose. It was the best of both worlds as far as she was concerned.

Why, though, did Piero choose to work through an agency instead of freelance? As a photographer, he could definitely make more money on his own. She'd have to ask him someday.

In the meantime, though, she needed to get ready to meet with her supervisor in New York and debrief about the recent assignments. As one of the senior members of the traveling teams, Felicity was asked to evaluate the shoots and everyone who worked them. Not everybody was cut out for the type of work they did, and the agency was keen on keeping their traveling teams booked to capacity and running smoothly. One person with the wrong attitude could throw an entire shoot off schedule, and problems like that snowballed and impacted every other shoot on the schedule.

On the bright side, New York was only a short train ride away from the nation's capital. She'd be able to spend a few days with her folks before she had to fly out for Scotland.

Felicity's phone beeped.

"Who's that, dear?" Her mom raised an eyebrow. "Your phone's been quite vocal, more so than usual."

"Leave her be, Martha. She's a grown woman. She can have phone friends if she wants."

"Of course she can have phone friends. I'm just surprised…"

Dinner with her folks. She loved them, and they loved her. Her mom had a way with words, though. Felicity's dad had once told her that her mom's own insecurities fueled the things she occasionally said to her daughter. Over the years, she'd been able to see how right he was and had learned not to read more into her mom's comments than what was there.

Even so, she occasionally bounced a comment back to her mom just to see her reaction. "Surprised I have a phone friend? Or surprised I have a friend at all?"

Her mom's face flooded with color. "I didn't mean it like that."

Felicity's dad rolled his eyes, but not before he said, "Daughter…"

"Sorry, Mom. I'm teasing."

Martha von Wolff pointed her fork at her daughter. "You're trying to get out of answering my question. That's what you're doing."

Youch. Despite their different perspectives, her mom could still read her better than anyone. "Maybe."

"What's his name?"

Felicity had no intention of opening that door. "Did I tell you guys about the tour I took of the Paris sewers…?"

Her dad threw back his head and laughed. "Your mom wants to know if you're dating anyone, and you bring up sewage. Now I've heard it all. If there is a guy, I can't wait to meet him."

Hm. Perhaps her change of subject had backfired…

Felicity's stomach was tied in knots as she walked off the plane in Cardiff. She was supposed to meet Piero, and then together they were meeting Rachel for lunch. Piero's plane had been delayed, though, and so she was going to be meeting a complete stranger on her own. Not any stranger, either. Piero's newly discovered cousin that even he didn't know particularly well.

A sigh slipped out. Nobody had promised that life would be

sunshine and roses, true. But meeting a complete stranger in an airport she wasn't terribly familiar with? Next time, she would make sure she was on the same plane as Piero.

Which implied there would be a next time... and somehow that thought didn't bother her quite as much as it would have a few weeks ago.

Felicity got through security and into the main concourse of the airport. With absolutely no idea what Rachel looked like, she had very little hope of finding the woman in the packed airport.

"Felicity...?"

Her head snapped up. A slender woman with wavy brown hair stood about three feet away, a hesitant smile shaping her lips and a question in her eyes.

"Are you Felicity?"

She nodded. "Rachel?"

The woman's shoulders released some of their tension. "Yeah. Piero texted to say he was running late but that you'd be here on time."

"How did you find me?"

Rachel flipped her phone around and showed Felicity the picture.

"When did he take that? I don't remember him taking any pictures of me."

Piero's cousin laughed before flicking her finger across the screen to show the dozen or so pictures of Felicity that he'd sent her. "He said he wanted to make sure I didn't miss you, but I think he just wanted to show you off."

"It's not like that..."

Rachel shook her head. "I may not know my new cousin very well, but I know people, artists especially. He wouldn't spend that much time finding you through the viewfinder if it wasn't like that."

CHAPTER SEVENTEEN

PIERO DISEMBARKED AND MADE HIS way through the crowded airport.

His baggage was being transferred automatically to his next flight, so no need to worry about that. He just needed to find...

Ah. There they were.

When he was two feet away, he dropped his carry-on bag by his feet, stepped forward, picked Felicity up by the waist, and twirled her around before setting her back on her feet. "You're a sight for sore eyes." Then he gave her the traditional European greeting, a kiss on each cheek. He didn't bother with the uber-polite air-kiss, though. He went for the real thing.

Man, it was good to see her. To catch the scent of her soap when he pulled her close and to let the sunshine in her eyes wash over him. Shock, too. And maybe a touch of disapproval. He'd surprised her, after all. He would focus on the sunshine, though, and the way she leaned into their embrace.

He released Felicity against his better judgment and turned to

Rachel. He pulled her close for a quick hug and a kiss on each cheek. They weren't quite at the air-twirl phase, though, so he skipped that part, especially since she stiffened in his embrace. She must be a prickly one.

Rachel laughed even if her eyes remained wary. "Follow me. The airport has a decent little café that serves coffee and sandwiches."

Within a few minutes, they were sitting elbow-to-elbow at a small table, each nursing a drink. Hot coffee for him, iced coffee for Felicity, and a properly British cup of hot tea for Rachel.

"So…" Rachel seemed as much at a loss now as she had been in Tuscany.

Piero was good at drawing people out, though. If he'd gotten Felicity to agree to meet him in Cardiff, he could surely handle one wayward cousin. "We didn't get a chance to talk much in Italy. Tell me what you do, what your life is like, if you're dating. Are there any men I should threaten for dumping you? I don't mind."

Nerves vibrated in Rachel's laugh, but the strain in her eyes eased, and the tight hold she had on her posture began to relax. "I teach secondary school art. My life is simple. I have my mom and my friends. No threats needed at present."

Felicity leaned forward. "You teach art? This whole painting thing must fascinate you, then. Have you gotten one yet?"

Rachel's lips tightened, and her eyes narrowed. She answered Felicity, but her eyes remained on Piero. "No, but I've been following on the family text and looking at the pictures of the ones that have been received so far. Whatever those paintings are about, I doubt I'll get one. Nobody really knows I exist."

Was it just him, or was Rachel bitter? She had a right to be upset, given all the water under the family bridge, but she hadn't been this stiff in Italy. Withdrawn, yes. Cautious, even. But not like this. Was there something else going on? Time to stick his toe in the water and see if he could figure it out. "Do you hear much from anybody in the family?"

Rachel visibly stiffened. "Not much. What about you?"

He shrugged. "All the time."

Rachel folded the napkin in front of her place at the small table. "Have you talked to Rafaele lately?"

"Rafaele? No, not lately. Should I have?"

His cousin's shoulders relaxed, and some of the wariness in her eyes seeped away. Maybe he needed to check in with Rafaele more often. Whatever was going on with Rachel, he'd bet anything his eldest cousin was at the center of it. Although... hm. With Rachel on the scene, Rafaele was no longer the oldest of his cousins.

"Do you have any ideas about where they're coming from? The paintings?" Thank goodness Felicity was keeping the conversation moving because he was at a loss, still stuck on the mind trip about Rachel now being the oldest of his cousins.

Rachel shook her head. "I'm the least likely to know. I mean, it seems like a family thing, and until this past spring, I didn't even know I had a family. But..."

Piero leaned in, too. She had his full attention. "But what?"

Rachel shrugged. "It might be nothing, but there's something familiar about the paintings. I feel like I should know the artist, but..."

"Me too!" Felicity's enthusiasm spilled over. "The brush strokes. The shadows. The use of color. There's something there. It's on the tip of my tongue, but I can't quite find it. I'm positive I've seen this artist before, but I can't place where."

Rachel gave Felicity a genuine smile, the last of her reservations seeming to melt away. "You've studied art?"

Felicity answered with a nod. "I started out in art history before I gravitated to theatrical cosmetic art."

Rachel's brow furrowed.

"I'm a makeup artist. For magazine spreads, mostly, but my major was focused on doing makeup for stage productions."

Rachel looked between them both. "Oh. That must be how you two met."

Piero frowned. "Didn't I tell you? That's why we're both passing through Cardiff. We have a shoot starting in Scotland."

His cousin gave a delicate shrug. "I knew that's why *you* were going to be here. Until this moment, all I knew about Felicity is that she's photogenic. You didn't exactly include captions with the photos you sent."

Heat inched its way up Piero's neck. "Yeah, well. I can't be expected to remember everything."

Rachel's eyes laughed at him before she cast a glance in Felicity's direction. "I like Piero. He makes me laugh. I only just met this whole, big family, and if I'm being honest, they're all terribly intimidating."

"Tell me about it."

"That's right. You got dialed in on the family text, didn't you? Because Piero's painting ended up in your hands."

Felicity grimaced. "The painting is intriguing, but the hundred texts a day can be a bit much."

"It's not…" Piero's sputter came to an end. He pulled out his phone, scrolled through something, and grimaced. "Okay. Maybe it is a hundred."

Felicity held her hand up to the side of her mouth as if trying to block him from reading her lips. Then she whispered loudly. "It's like being stalked en masse."

Rachel ignored his eye roll and continued chatting with Felicity. "Has he told you what any of his cousins do for a living? Or his brothers, for that matter?"

Felicity shook her head.

Rachel leaned back in her chair and started ticking them off on her fingers. "Life-saving firefighter, pizza chain entrepreneur, music composer, and lawyer, to name a few. And here I am. A teacher. I don't exactly fit in."

Felicity's eyes had widened with each new revelation until they looked like they were ready to swallow her face.

Piero needed to take control of this conversation. Thank goodness time was flying. "I hate to break this up…"

Felicity swiped at her phone to see the clock. "Wow. I thought we still had an hour. I guess we need to get going."

They all rose from their table and made their way toward the airport's security checkpoint.

"It was good to see you again, Piero. And I'm glad I could meet you, Felicity."

"Same here." Felicity's smile brightened the airport.

How was he supposed to say goodbye to someone he hardly knew? "I'll let you know the next time I'm passing through. Maybe I can make it an overnight and we can have more time."

Rachel nodded. "I'd like that." And it looked like she meant it. Her shoulders were relaxed, and her expression was open — the complete opposite of when he'd greeted her.

He started to step away before turning back and pulling Rachel into a hug. "I'm glad you're in the family. I know it'll take some getting used to, but the family will be richer for having you."

"Thank you." She returned his embrace and whispered in his ear, "You need to tell her how you feel. Felicity's a keeper."

Piero stepped away, nodded to Rachel, and ushered Felicity toward the security line. As soon as they made it through, he turned back and gave Rachel one last wave. Then he captured Felicity's hand in his. "Come on. Scotland's going to be fantastic."

Was Rachel right? Should he tell Felicity how he felt? He hadn't exactly kept it a secret, but he hadn't been explicit, either. Would he be going too fast if he laid all his cards on the table? If he pushed too far, too soon, she might run screaming toward the hills.

He glanced sideways at her.

The truth was, he'd spent enough of his life fitting into the role he'd created for himself, a role designed to keep people at arm's length. Now that he'd met someone he wanted to pull closer, he was afraid that if he let his need show, the illusion would shatter.

Could he live with the consequences if that happened?

CHAPTER EIGHTEEN

WAS IT POSSIBLE TO FALL in love after only one date?

Technically, they'd only shared one date. That day between jobs in Paris.

One look into his eyes when he wasn't wearing the veneer of his career, and Felicity had been lost.

She hadn't wanted to admit it then.

So what was different now?

Piero held her hand and jogged toward the gate so they could catch their plane, and all she could think about was the time they'd just spent with Rachel.

That day in Paris, she'd seen Piero the man. No façade, no playboy persona. Just Piero.

And with Rachel? It had been the same. Piero the man.

Maybe a little bit of Piero the cousin, but even then, it hadn't felt like an act.

Could she fall in love after just one date?

No. Not possible.

She could, however, fall far enough to start thinking the L-word no longer seemed like a far-fetched fantasy.

And that was a scary enough proposition to steal her breath away.

Turbulence threatened to bring Felicity's coffee back to the surface.

Piero reached over and took her hand in his.

She glanced at him.

Cad.

He was completely at ease, his face relaxed and calm.

"Can I get you something?"

She shook her head and gritted her teeth.

His thumb traced along the back of her hand in a repeating motion starting in the center and working out in different directions. He applied enough pressure to be soothing.

"I don't normally mind flying."

His smile filled the periphery of her vision. "This ride is rougher than most."

"You're not bothered by it?"

He shrugged. "It gives me an excuse to hold your hand."

A smile tugged the corners of her lips upward as Felicity closed her eyes and focused on his touch on her hand. It was hypnotic in a way. Relaxing, too. When she focused on Piero's thumb on her hand, the flight didn't seem nearly as bumpy.

Settled into her hotel room for the night, Felicity booted up her computer and checked her email. A message from Rachel awaited her.

It was great to meet you Felicity. I hope that won't be a one-off. If you think of anything concerning the paintings, let me know. If you can narrow it down to any names, I'd love to be able to check them out as well. Maybe between the two of us – the ones who are new to the family and maybe more objective? – we can figure this whole thing out.

Blessings!
Rachel

Hm. *New to the family.* She wasn't quite sure what to do with that. She wasn't in the family. Not the way Rachel was, anyway. But still. It was a nice sentiment, especially coming from Rachel. She hadn't gotten the impression that Piero's cousin was normally the outgoing type.

Felicity closed her email and opened a browser. She needed to take a virtual tour of some artwork. Maybe something she saw would jog her memory and help her figure out why Piero's painting was so familiar to her.

A light tap at Felicity's door the next morning drew her attention from the computer screen she'd been staring at for the past five minutes. "Who's there?"

"Your knight in shining armor."

Hm. Knight, indeed. She still wasn't sure about this guy. Piero was… He was a lot more than she'd ever given him credit for. That was true. But this new understanding of him didn't entirely negate her previous impression of him. As much as she liked Piero the man, she wasn't yet convinced that Piero the player was entirely fictional.

"Um… Are you going to open the door?"

Whoops. "Sorry!" The scent of seasoned sausage met her as she pulled the door open. "Mm… That smells good."

He bowed with a flourish of his arm, managing to keep the bag upright the entire time. "Bangers and tattie scones. Protein and golden-fried carbs. Delicious." On his way back to upright, he lifted a cardboard cup carrier from the floor.

"Coffee?"

"But of course. I'm aiming for knighthood, after all."

Felicity reached for the coffee, but he pulled it out of her reach. "Rules, m'lady. Care to follow me down to the lobby?"

She glanced at her still-open computer. "Um…"

CHAPTER NINETEEN

PIERO PEEKED OVER HER SHOULDER. Something on that laptop was tempting her away from fresh, hot coffee. It must be important. "Don't tell me you're a social media junkie."

She took the few steps over to the computer, snapped the lid closed, and slipped into her sneakers. "I told Rachel I'd look at some paintings, so I was checking out different art museums online to see if I could find a string to pull at."

"You never cease to amaze me."

She reached for a coffee as they approached the elevator. "What makes you say that?"

"I got a call last night. A couple of calls, actually. One was from Nonna, but we'll save that for another time. The one I'm talking about now was from a photo editor I worked with on a project a few years back. He needed me to run through the shots from an old shoot. He remembered a particular photo he wanted to use, but because it wasn't one that made it into the magazine spread the first time around, he hadn't kept the shot. He was going off of memory. And his description was... fuzzy. So I had to go through the entire shoot to see if I could find one poorly described photo."

She took a sip of her steaming coffee. "Sounds like a headache."

"Yeah, but it's part of the job. And sometimes I find hidden gems when I do that. Last night, for example."

Her attention seemed to be on her coffee more than it was on him. "Yeah?"

"I didn't realize we'd worked together before Dresden."

Ah. Now he had her attention. Her eyes widened before she looked away. So she *had* known they'd worked together before. But she hadn't mentioned it. The woman was perplexing.

Felicity shook her head as the elevator continued its descent. "I'm not convinced you're the same person now that you were then."

What did that have to do with why she didn't mention it? "What do you mean?"

She lifted a shoulder. "I always thought you were too much of a flirt and always looking for a fun time, so I avoided you. I'm not the flirty or fun kind of girl."

"I think you're fun." And a little flirty, but he kept that thought to himself.

"Maybe. I'm not sure I used to be, though. Let's face it. Prior to Paris, I had a pretty unfavorable opinion of you. But I didn't always have a good attitude about the modeling world, either, and that may have affected the way I saw people."

"What kind of attitude did you have?"

A blush colored her cheeks. "I was a stick in the mud."

"Not a phrase I would ever use to describe you."

They exited the elevator and made their way toward one of the tables scattered around the edges of the lobby. "Thanks. But back then? I was...a little too judgmental. Part of me was worried that the career I'd chosen would present me with too much temptation, you know? So I overcorrected, and in the process, I became judgmental of others. God's always working on me, though, and this is one of the areas He's been teaching me about this past year. If we'd met back then, I'm not sure you would have thought I was worth a second glance. But then, I think you're a different person now than back then, too."

Was different good...or bad? "In what way?"

She took the paper-wrapped sausage Piero held out to her. "Well... For starters, I think you really were a playboy back then."

He lifted an eyebrow as he arranged the tattie scones — something similar to an American potato cake — on the napkin between them. "I thought we'd settled that misconception."

"I agree that you don't seem like a playboy now, but I think you were back then. I think you went out with all the different models — even if you never did anything inappropriate with them — because you relished the reputation you were building. You had fun, and you looked forward to being out on the town with a beautiful woman on your arm every night. I think that had already changed by the time we bumped into each other in Dresden."

He gave her a full wattage smile. "It was a bit more than a bump."

The corner of her mouth tilted up. "Now you're avoiding the subject."

"I'm not convinced you could ever be a stick in the mud, but you might be right about me. The random dating scene hadn't been much fun for a while. I just thought I was getting bored, though. Restless for a change."

"I suppose that could be it." She popped the last bite into her mouth.

He stared at her mouth for a second too long, long enough for it to capture his imagination. What would her lips feel like against his? He forced himself to look away, out across the lobby, before taking a drink of his coffee and returning his attention to her. "I recently came to understand that some of the relationship choices I've made as an adult have been shaped by something that happened when I was just barely a man. And that's not the life I want for myself."

She studied him across the table, her brows drawn together. "For someone who I thought of as painfully transparent, you're suddenly all murky. What happened?"

He smiled reflexively, the kind of smile you gave when uncomfortable with what you were saying but didn't want the other person to realize it. "My mom died the summer before I headed off to college. Ovarian cancer."

Felicity's face paled. "My best friend in high school lost an aunt to ovarian cancer. I don't know much about the disease. Except that it's fast-moving and almost always fatal. I'm sorry."

"Yeah. Me, too."

She leaned forward like she was about to say something. Then she reversed her momentum and leaned back. She reached for her coffee. Then put it down again. "And how did that affect your relationship choices?"

"Mom was Italian."

Felicity squinted at him. "Italian matters because…?"

A bark of laughter escaped. "She was Italian, and she was my mom. That meant she was involved in every part of my life, and I wasn't allowed to keep secrets from her. She was nosy, and she was amazing, and her opinion mattered to me more than I ever let her know. She asked a million questions about every girl I ever dated."

"She sounds special."

"She was. I didn't realize it at the time. I wasn't old enough to, I guess. But later on, it was kind of like every woman I dated needed

Mom's approval. But she wasn't there to give it…"

"So settling down was officially off the table."

He stood and collected their empty cups. Anything to avoid eye contact. "Crazy, right?"

Felicity rose, too, and reached out, resting a hand on Piero's arm. "Not crazy. A little misguided, maybe. But also noble and a little bit adorable."

He set their empty cups back down on the table, covered her hand with his own, and leaned in. Before his mind had time to register what he was planning to do, his lips brushed against her cheek. Her skin was warm and soft, electric and inviting. And alarming. His heartrate kicked into overdrive, and heat began to coalesce in his midsection. This was nothing like the greeting he'd given her at the airport in Cardiff. Those cheek-kisses had been friendly. He'd kept them that way on purpose. This kiss, though, had gotten away from him before he'd even realized he'd intended to kiss her.

And it was so much more than friendly.

He was in trouble. If a kiss on her cheek could have his fingers itching to curl into her hair, then he needed to avoid a kiss on the lips at all cost. Or she would tempt him to do something none of the models he'd ever dated had been able to get him to do… cross the threshold and into her room.

Not that Felicity would invite him to. Not intentionally, anyway.

She was right in a way. The modeling world was full of temptation. It had just taken him until now to come face-to-face with it.

Had Rachel been right? Should he tell Felicity how he felt? And after Nonna's call…

Piero pulled away, regathered their garbage, and carried it over to a nearby receptacle. He took his time, pulled in some deep breaths, and tried to shake away the emotions tangling up his brain before he turned back to her. "Anything specific you want to see? We can wander aimlessly or get one of those guided tour maps."

She blinked at him. Then she blinked again. "Um...a map? Or aimlessly. I, um... Either is fine."

Well then. He wasn't the only one affected by that kiss, and knowing that made his step lighter and his smile wider. "Let's ask at the front desk."

CHAPTER TWENTY

THE MORNING HAD SPED BY. Armed with a map and advice from the front desk clerk about which sites were usually mobbed by tourists, Felicity and Piero had enjoyed a touristy — but not too touristy — morning. They'd managed to take in two historical sites and a couple of art galleries.

"I'm starving." Felicity slid into a booth at the pub someone at the museum had recommended.

Piero slipped into the seat opposite hers. "You and me both. Who knew not working could work up such an appetite?"

She picked up her menu — a small piece of paper sitting on the edge of the table — and wished for a big American menu to hide behind. She was discovering another side of Piero, a funny and entertaining side, and she hadn't quite figured out what to do about it yet.

In Paris, she'd realized he was kinder and more thoughtful than she'd ever given him credit for, and that he could be serious, too. In Cardiff, she'd seen a caring cousin trying to help strengthen family bonds. Now in Kelso, she was finding out about his quirky sense of humor. Not to mention the way he could set her world on fire with a kiss to her cheek. Piero was a walking, talking billboard for danger.

And yet…each time she learned something new about him, she liked him a little bit more. Or a lot. She'd better not go down that road, or she'd be daydreaming about more kisses and sighing like a silly schoolgirl.

"What c'n I git fer ye?" The waitress stood there staring at her.

"Uh…bangers and mash?"

The waitress chuckled. "American, eh?"

Piero set his menu down on the table. "What do you recommend?"

The woman pointed to the menu. "Most Americans lach anything aboon this line. If y' want tae gang below th' line, Ah'd recommend th' flamin' kilt burger m'self. Or th' highlan' burger."

Piero's eyebrow lifted. "What do you think?"

Felicity shrugged. "I'm game if you are."

"We'll take one of each and two Irn-Brus."

The waitress turned away, shouted their order in the general direction of the kitchen, and moved on to another table.

Piero drummed his fingers on the menu before speaking. "I didn't mean to stop you from ordering."

Goodness, that man was complex. "Was I supposed to be bothered by that?"

He moved the menu back to the edge of the table where it had started. "Women sometimes like to be independent. They don't like being rescued."

She chuckled. "That kind of rescue I can handle. I had no idea what to order. I hadn't even read the menu yet. I said the first thing that came to mind and hoped it was something they served."

"You could have told her you needed more time."

"Didn't you hear the part where I said I'm starving? I don't think straight when I'm hungry. I'm cranky without my coffee in the morning, and I'm loopy any time I don't get food."

He leaned back in the booth. "Loopy, huh? So if I ever want you to agree to something you'd normally say no to, I should withhold food first."

She picked up her fork and jabbed it into the air between them. "Them's fighting words, mister."

Piero moves his glass out of range of her fork. "Have you had Irn-Bru before?"

"You can't come to Scotland and not try one. I like it well-enough. I generally prefer water with meals, though."

The waitress chose that moment to stop back by their table to deliver their drinks. She started to move on without a word, but Piero stopped her. "And a water for the lady, please."

The waitress offered a brisk nod before walking off.

Piero took a sip of his drink. "Hunger aside, there are times when you don't want to be rescued. That's what it sounded like, anyway."

"Sure. We all have our idiosyncrasies."

"You could make it easy on me and just tell me about your idiosyncrasies now so I don't step on your toes later."

Funny man. As if it was that simple. "Most of us don't recognize our idiosyncrasies until we're in the middle of them. And even then, we don't always acknowledge them. And it's not like I can instantly recall every time I've been bothered by someone taking charge of a situation."

Piero shook his head. "You're not making this easy for me."

"This?"

His lids dropped to half-mast. "Courtship."

"'ere ye go." The waitress set the glass of water down and disappeared again before anyone could thank her.

Felicity's heart couldn't decide whether to stall out or race at top speed. "C-c…"

"Courtship. You can say it."

"I didn't know that's what we were doing."

"Nonna called last night. My cousins have been tattling on me. She wanted to know about the pretty American I've been courting and whether or not you'll be accompanying me to Tuscany in September."

"September?" Such a great time for her ability to speak independent thoughts to abandon her.

"Then she gave me this whole lecture about how she's not getting any younger and would like to see her playboy grandson settle down, but if I think she's putting us in the same room, I will know wrath like I've never known before. Or something like that."

Forget her confused heart. Heat flamed to life in Felicity's face. "Same room?"

He winked at her. "Anyway. Courtship. It was Nonna's word. I just thought we were dating. Are we dating? Exclusively, I mean. Or are you just using me for my good looks and charming ways?"

His voice said he was teasing, but his eyes… They said her answer mattered a great deal. So… yet another new side of Piero Carter that she hadn't seen before. Uncertainty. Or maybe insecurity? Was insecurity supposed to be sexy? Because it was. On him, at least.

Felicity reached for her water glass and gripped it with both hands. Talking was easier when her hands were occupied, which was one of the reasons she did well as a makeup artist but utterly failed in most social settings. "I guess I thought maybe we were getting to know each other…?"

"Which is how many steps shy of actually dating?"

"Um… Is that important?"

Piero stared over her left shoulder for a second or two before his

116

gaze returned to her face. "Are you asking me to be patient, or are you telling me not to get my hopes up?"

Why did they need to have this talk now? Couldn't they just enjoy the day and each other's company? Flirt a little?

Then again, flirting generally led to other things... like conversations about where relationships were going.

Felicity tucked a stray strand of hair behind her ear. "I guess I don't know. I wasn't thinking ahead. I was just enjoying myself."

A smile lit his eyes. "Isn't that one of your early complaints against me? That I didn't take things seriously and was only out for a good time?"

And there went her blush again. The heat didn't bother climbing inch by inch. It flooded her face all at once. She must look like she was about to combust. "Maybe..."

He reached across and nudged one of her hands free from her glass. His grip wasn't tight, but he intertwined his fingers with hers. "I'm probably getting what I deserve. For years, I had no interest in a serious relationship. Now that I've met someone who makes me think it would be worth the time and effort, worth the investment, I'm stuck. I've fallen for a woman who's skittish about trusting a man who's never taken a relationship seriously."

Her heart turned over. "I like you."

"And I like you. A lot."

"I need time, though, more than I need pressure."

He gave a solemn nod. "I can handle that."

"Would you have brought this up if your nonna hadn't called you last night?"

The corner of his mouth tilted up in the most delicious way. "Good point. I probably would have kept my mouth shut and followed your lead."

"I want to trust you."

Shadows moved into his eyes, making them midnight dark. "Is

that what it comes down to?"

"Sort of."

"Have I given you any reason not to trust me?"

The waitress chose that moment to set their plates down, forcing their hands apart. The distance felt more than just physical. She shouldn't have used the T-word. It was a sore spot for him. One of those idiosyncrasies they'd talked about earlier, the kind people didn't usually realize about themselves.

Felicity waited for the waitress to leave. "I'm usually a pretty good judge of character, but you're turning out to be so different than I first thought, and that makes me cautious. Are you the man I see before me now, or are you the man I thought you were up until Dresden? I'm not sure, and that makes me question my own judgement. Worse, I'm still not sure that you're sure."

He reached for her other hand and held it loosely as he bowed his head. "Lord, thank You for this meal and the chance to explore this corner of the world. Thank You for Felicity and the special woman she is. We ask You to guide us both in this thing — the getting-to-know-each-other, or the dating, or whatever it is. We want Your will in our lives. Amen."

When Felicity looked up, the shadows were gone from Piero's eyes. Good. She didn't like being responsible for making him feel that way. She didn't want to let him down, either, and she didn't quite know what to do about the way her stomach had twisted at the thought of hurting him.

"So?" He threw the challenge down. "Are you going to take the first bite, or shall I? I understand if you're chicken…"

CHAPTER TWENTY-ONE

THAT WAS OFFICIALLY THE LAST time he was going to take his new cousin's advice.

Or let Nonna pressure him.

At least they had food in front of them, something to talk about beside the awkward exchange they'd just shared.

"So which one do you want?" Piero eyed the two burgers and awaited Felicity's response.

"Tell me again what we ordered...?"

He picked up the menu and glanced down at the bottom. "Ahh... Are you sure you want to know?"

She winced.

"One is a burger topped with black pudding, and the other is a burger with haggis on it."

She winced again. "I should have stayed above the line."

He pushed the plate with the black pudding burger toward her. "That one's easier to take off if you don't want it."

Felicity picked up her burger and squared her shoulders before taking a bite. She chewed longer than seemed necessary, but she did eventually swallow it down.

"So? How was it?"

"It might taste good if I didn't know what went into the pudding. As it is, I had to fight the urge to gag. I'm all for trying authentic local cuisine, but next time, could you pick something that doesn't have blood as a main ingredient?"

"It's all in your head. If you don't think about it, you'll be fine."

She shook her head like a parent humoring a toddler. "Of course it's in my head. The problem is, I can't get out of my head." Then she shook a finger at his burger. "Now try your haggis burger."

This probably wasn't the best time to tell her he'd had haggis before and didn't mind it. He didn't seek it out, but if it was served to him, he enjoyed it. He took a big bite of his burger and watched her eyes narrow. Oops. He'd been found out.

"Let me guess. You don't like black pudding."

Piero gave her a half-shrug. "It's not my favorite."

Her shoe started tapping under the table.

"Um… Do you want to trade?" He offered her the haggis burger.

With deft fingers, she slipped the pudding patty off of her burger, stared at it a second, then reached for a napkin to cover it. Once done, she picked up her burger and smiled. "It might be all in my head, but if I'm not careful, it'll end up all over your shoes."

The woman was daring. He knew that from working with her. She wasn't weak, afraid, or timid. She had the weakest stomach of anyone he'd ever met, though. Felicity was the definition of contradiction.

"Are you ready for tomorrow's shoot?" Piero had been looking forward to this shoot ever since it had showed up on his calendar.

They walked back toward the hotel the agency had booked for the shoot staff. "Floors Castle? I've wanted to visit it for years. I can't wait."

"It looks like we'll have some fantastic locations on the estate, too. Not just the castle."

She sighed. "The gardens are supposed to be amazing. I looked at them online, but a computer screen can't do something like that justice."

"Not the way a printed photo can?"

She nudged him with her elbow. "Are you fishing for compliments?"

Piero laughed. "A photographer took the picture you saw online, so I'm not sure that counts as fishing. You're right, though. Online pictures somehow seem more two-dimensional than their printed counterparts."

"Is that why you don't have an online portfolio?"

His step slowed. "You looked for my portfolio?"

She gave a small shrug. "I was curious."

"Should I be flattered?"

"Not if you know what's good for you."

Piero waved his arm wide. "Isn't it a beautiful night sky?"

"You're avoiding the question. What gives?"

"Most of my work is contracted through the agency. I can't post it separate from them."

"Yeah, but I've seen you. You take pictures all the time. Right now you have a small camera tucked away in your pocket. You've been snapping away all day whenever you've thought I wasn't paying attention."

Heat climbed his neck. "I'm not used to being figured out like this."

"Rachel having a dozen pics of me on her phone kind of clued me in. I was oblivious till then. You have a picture of me in Rodin's sculpture garden. From Paris. How did I not see you take pictures that day?"

"I'm sneaky like that?"

"But why?" Felicity stepped in front of him and faced him with hands on her hips. "Why hide the fact that you take pictures? You're a photographer. I don't get it."

Piero rubbed the back of his neck. "It's complicated."

"So, explain it."

"I love photography. Taking pictures is as much a part of me as eating or breathing."

"That makes sense."

"People sometimes give me odd looks when I walk around with a camera hanging from my neck. It's usually okay, but it can get awkward. Especially if I'm caught up in the moment and the scene and what I'm doing."

"Okay...? It's not like you're the self-conscious type. I still don't get it."

"I... Um... It's difficult to explain." His hand, already in his pocket, instinctively clutched his camera.

Felicity dropped her hands to her sides. "Is it about me?"

He blinked. He would have rather she asked if that dress made her look fat. He could have honestly told her it hugged her in all the right places and made her look like a movie star. This, though? "You and I are different people."

She nodded.

"I don't mind people staring at me or wondering what I'm doing. It doesn't faze me."

"But I'm self-conscious..."

"I didn't want you to feel weird if people stared or pointed or anything like that."

"Oh."

"It's not a big deal."

She turned around and started walking again.

"Does this mean you're mad at me or that we're okay?"

She glanced over her shoulder. "I'm still deciding."

"When do you think you'll make up your mind?"

"When I'm ready."

Great. He'd brought up the word *courtship* at lunch, and that had been a disaster. Now this. Could the day get any worse?

Then her laugh reached back and tickled his ears. "Made up your mind yet?"

"I suppose."

He sped up his pace to make up the distance between them. "And?"

"I forgive you."

Had he actually done anything wrong?

"Stop treating me like glass, though. I have hang-ups, sure."

"Like sewers."

She sighed. "Yes, apparently like sewers. But I'm not spending every minute waiting for you to say or do the wrong thing. I know I said I used to be a stick-in-the-mud, but I'm not *that* uptight."

"I never meant to imply…"

"Ask next time. 'Will it make you uncomfortable if…?' It can't be that hard to say."

It was his turn to sigh. "You're probably right."

"Probably?"

Piero shook his head. This woman who had captured his imagination was as unpredictable as they came. The second he thought he had her figured out, she did a one-eighty and shocked him in a new way.

For a man who liked adventure and abhorred boredom, she could easily become an addiction.

CHAPTER TWENTY-TWO

COULD PIERO BE ANY MORE confusing? Or was she really that sensitive? It was perfectly okay and right for Felicity to be offended that he felt the need to tip-toe around her feelings.

Right?

Or was she losing it?

Because, while she was bothered by that, she also found it — and Piero — to be sweet.

Piero was misguided, yes. He was also a gentleman, though.

Which brought Felicity back to where she started. Could Piero be any more confusing?

Felicity shook the thoughts away and concentrated on the person in her chair. "Iceland, huh? At least it's summer."

Patrice laughed. "It was breathtaking, but I'm not sure there's enough money to get me there during the winter."

"I've always heard that Iceland is green and Greenland is full of ice."

"You could find out. There's a gig in Greenland coming up in

September. You should sign up for it."

"Are you going?"

"I keep a map where I mark off the different countries I've been to. I want to hit as many as I can before I retire."

"Retire? You're not old enough to be thinking about retirement."

Patrice's head bobbed. "Oh, sweetheart, you are good for the soul. Modeling's a girl's game, though, and I left girlhood behind a while ago. It won't be much longer before I start to get fewer and fewer calls, before someone tells me I'm not quite right for a particular shoot. I love what I do, but I do it with my eyes open."

"You're not like the others. I hope you stick around for a long time to come."

The model waved her comment away with a delicate hand. "Tell me about Piero. Are the two of you finally on speaking terms?"

Felicity's skin heated.

One of Patrice's eyebrows arched. "Do tell."

"It's nothing."

"You have milk-white skin, dear. You couldn't hide a blush if you tried."

Felicity reached for the palette that would help her to give Patrice the soft, romantic look that morning's shoot called for. "He's not quite like I originally thought."

The model managed to snort without moving a single facial muscle.

"Hey. It's not my fault I thought he was a player."

"Has he taken you out yet?"

"Uh... I guess?"

"You guess?" Patrice rolled her eyes. "What does that even mean?"

"We toured the Paris sewers."

The model shoved Felicity's hand away from her face and started laughing. "Oh, dear. The sewers? He must be off his game. Piero's usually way more romantic than that."

Felicity waited for Patrice's laughter to subside before returning to her work. "We also visited an art museum and had lunch in a sculpture garden."

"That sounds more like the Piero I know."

"How well do you know him?"

"Officially? We've been on two dates, both in public venues where I wanted to be seen, and he didn't mind being on my arm to help me accomplish that."

Tightness coiled in Felicity's belly. "And unofficially?"

A barely there shrug, followed by words spoken so softly that Felicity had to lean in and concentrate to hear. "Piero and I realized a few things about each other. Neither of us was interested in a relationship with the other, and we both have an affinity for family and God. That opened a few doors for an off-the-record friendship. We keep in touch. He accompanied me to a funeral of an old friend because I didn't want to go alone. He swears funerals don't count, though, so he's never broken his two-date rule with me."

"You're a believer?"

"Don't be so surprised."

"I'm not." Felicity put the finishing touches on Patrice's face before reaching for the model's hair. The hair stylist was backed up, so she was helping out. "You make better sense to me now."

"Was I confusing before?"

"You're a model, and you're nice."

"The two don't have to be mutually exclusive."

Heat climbed Felicity's neck again. "I know, and it's not. I've met several kind models in my career. You're just the most consistent about it, and you don't turn into some sort of she-monster when a shoot goes badly and you get blamed for it."

"Piero's not the type to blame the model unless they deserve it."

"I'm not talking about him."

"Yeah, well. I'm glad. He's one of the good ones. A little misguided at times, but still good."

Why did a conversation that should be happy feel so awkward? "I'm a believer, too."

"I kind of figured."

"Why don't we ever talk about it? I've known you over a year, and this has never come up before? It should have. I mean, I should have said something before now. I should..."

Patrice leaned forward to give Felicity better access to the back of her hair. "You don't exactly talk about yourself. And it's not like I go around telling every person I meet that I love Jesus."

"Yeah, but..."

"Can't change the past. I suppose we could do something different going forward, though."

"Like what?" Felicity found her sassy streak and winked at Patrice in the mirror. "Tell everyone we meet that we love Jesus?"

Patrice grinned as much as she dared without risking the makeup job. "I was thinking smaller scale. Maybe have Bible study together whenever we're on the same shoot."

"That might be fun."

"*Might?* You sure know how to beat a girl's ego down."

Felicity twisted a final loop of hair into place and stepped back. "It's not my fault your ego is so fragile."

Patrice shook her head. "Where have you been hiding all this time? I swear I've done at least a dozen shoots with you and never realized you spoke my love language."

"Love language?"

"Sarcasm."

Felicity shook her head. She'd done quite a number on herself, hadn't she? Keeping everyone at arm's length by assuming nobody wanted anything to do with her outside of the makeup chair. "I'm not fluent yet, but I'm learning."

"I'm going to enjoy getting to know you better, Felicity von Wolff."

Sixteen-hour days took their toll on most people, but after three of them, Felicity was in a stupor. Their third day of shooting had come to a close, and she needed to pack up her supplies. A snail on a glue stick would have moved faster than her, though.

"Is this a bad time to tap my toe and point at my watch?" Even Piero's smile drooped at the edges, no doubt worn out from the long hours.

"If you tap, it might put me to sleep."

"Come on. Tell me what I can do to help."

She waved toward a table. "Those things all need to go in this case."

Piero looked from the pile of supplies on the table to the teeny, tiny case she packed it all into. "Makeup artist and magician?"

"One of my many super powers." Felicity opened the case and began tucking the supplies away, one at a time.

"I've caught you looking at me with a puzzled look more than once these last few days. Anything you want to share with me?"

He had to go and ask, didn't he? She had very little filter when she was this tired, and she wasn't sure she wanted him to know what was going on inside her head. "Every time I see a different side of you, I realize that I need to think about you in a new way."

"Is that bad?"

"Yes. Because you have lots of sides, and constantly reevaluating who I think you are is exhausting."

His brow drew together. "Why do I feel like I'm stepping in quicksand here?"

"Exactly my point. Remember that tourist who wandered onto the set yesterday?"

He nodded.

"He spoke some language nobody else here understood. People just wanted him gone. You took the time to talk to him, though, and to figure out what was wrong. You helped him."

"Which is good… Right?"

Felicity tucked a few more items away in her case. "Of course it's good. But it was a new side of you yet again. What language was that, anyway?"

"Not a clue. I ran through all the languages I know until I hit one he also sort-of spoke. He was just asking for directions. He didn't mean to disrupt the shoot."

"And the day before that, we were returning to the hotel late at night. Everyone was tired. Nobody noticed the man standing in the shadows of the hotel. Except for you. You're the only one who saw him, let alone did anything to help him."

Color crept up Piero's neck. "He was hungry. It was no big deal."

"How many of the crew are staying at the hotel?"

"Two dozen?"

"And you're the only one who saw him, the only one who wasn't so wrapped up in his own fatigue that he could notice someone else in need."

"You're making me sound like some kind of paragon, and I promise you, I'm not."

Felicity forced the last vial into her case and snapped it closed. "Don't worry. I rode a carpet with you in Dresden. I know you're not perfect. But I realized that I was thinking about you all wrong. That's probably why I was staring."

"Wrong how?" His question seemed to have a pulse of its own.

How was she still stringing words together? She had to be sleepwalking. "Instead of reorganizing the way I think about you each time I learn something new, I need to think about it in terms of layers. You have many layers, and each new layer I see adds something to the picture I have in my head of you. I don't need to erase the picture and start over. I just need to add the new layer and see where it takes me. Or takes the picture. Or... Uh... Does that make sense?"

Piero plucked the case from Felicity's hand and got a grip on her wheeled suitcase, too. "Come on. I'll drive you back to the hotel."

She crossed her arms and stood there. "You didn't answer my question."

"You know you're funny when you're tired, right?"

That was beside the point.

"Yes, you make sense. Fuzzy, sleepy sense, but sense nonetheless."

That was probably better than she deserved. Felicity followed behind Piero, her eyes focused downward so she didn't trip on the uneven ground.

"I don't suppose you're interested in dinner?"

"Unless that's code for sleep, no."

"Breakfast? Which I'm told is code for food-after-sleep."

"That's an offer I can accept."

Piero loaded Felicity's two cases next to his equipment in the trunk of his rental. "Your chariot awaits, m'lady."

She giggled. Actually giggled. "I shouldn't be allowed in public when I'm this tired."

Oye. No filter. Hopefully, Piero forgot this entire conversation.

CHAPTER TWENTY-THREE

PIERO KNOCKED ON FELICITY'S DOOR. She'd said she would meet him at nine, but it was going on ten, and she hadn't shown her face in the lobby yet. As out of it as she'd been the night before, she might still be sound asleep.

"Hey." She turned away as soon as she opened her door.

So… Not asleep.

Just not where she said she'd be.

Piero pushed her door the rest of the way in and leaned his back against it, one foot in her room and one foot technically still in the hallway. "You said nine."

She glanced up from her laptop but stared right through him. "Give me a sec."

He waited three minutes. That was a whole hundred and eighty seconds. Surely that was enough time to appear patient. "What're you working on?"

She waved a hand absently. "I told Rachel I'd look at something."

Rachel? "My cousin?"

She nodded, her eyes glued to her computer screen.

"Look at what?"

"Give me a sec."

Hadn't he already given her enough seconds? Not that he minded waiting all that much. She sat on her bed, angled toward the window — probably so the sun would hit the back of her screen and not the front. The image she created was a study in perfection. Just enough shadow to create mystery, and just enough light to give her an aura of innocence.

"Got it!" She pumped her fist.

"Whatever you're doing must be awfully engrossing."

Felicity grabbed her phone, did some fast two-thumbed typing on it, and then closed her laptop. She turned her smile on Piero, and the force of it nearly pushed him the rest of the way over the threshold. "You're awfully pleased with yourself."

She tucked her phone into a pocket, grabbed a small purse, and headed his way. "I woke up this morning with a clear idea of where I'd seen that painting style before."

Painting...? *Oh.* "Do you think you found the artist?"

"I took this summer seminar one year in college, and we looked at several contemporary painters. Like I said, I'm a Van Gogh girl, so when somebody of a different style grabs me, I take notice, and there were a handful of painters that summer whose paintings spoke to me."

"Figuratively, I hope...?"

She rolled her eyes at him as they waited for the elevator. "Anyway, when I woke up this morning, the name of the gallery was my first thought. How weird is that? I love the way God works things out like that."

"So you found the gallery online?"

"Yeah. We studied the paintings online because the gallery is in

134

Moscow."

Huh. Moscow. Not what he'd expected, but that didn't mean it wasn't important. He stared at her so long she reached past him to push the button for the lobby. The elevator doors closed before he found his voice. "You have my attention."

"There were about a dozen similar artists that summer. It was for a special showing the gallery was doing. I don't remember the name of the showing. In looking at their site just now, I recognized three of the names, though. The styles, too."

"They match the paintings my family's been getting?"

The doors opened, and they stepped into the lobby. "Sort of. They're similar. Close enough that I think it's worth a second opinion, and Rachel's probably just the person to give that opinion."

"Straight to her? Not in the group text?"

"Yeah..."

What wasn't she telling him? "Any particular reason?"

She stared at her shoes.

"You can tell me. I probably won't be offended."

She glanced up and then away. "It's just that your family's really overwhelming, and I got the feeling from Rachel that she wasn't totally comfortable with them. It's not so much what she said. Just... I don't know. A private text seemed better. More friendly, too. She either finds something, or she doesn't. She doesn't need your family breathing down her neck about it, though."

Piero reached out and hooked a finger under Felicity's chin, tilting her face toward his. "I think that's perfect. Thank you for thinking of her feelings."

She gave the tiniest of nods, the look in her eyes somewhere between dreamy and wary.

How was a guy supposed to process those kinds of mixed signals? He leaned down and gave her a light kiss on the forehead before stepping away. "Do you still want breakfast, or should we head out to see more of the sights?"

Piero held Felicity's chair for her before seating himself. A light breakfast, followed by a morning traipsing through old abbeys, lent itself to a hearty appetite. Lunch should be fabulous, although they were both likely to read the menu a little closer this time.

"I think it's a serve yourself place." Felicity pointed toward the bar. Customers were lining up to give their drink orders.

"What would you like?"

"Iced tea, if they have it. Otherwise, just water."

"With lemon?"

"Of course."

As he stood in the slow-moving line, a woman sidled up behind him. "You from around here?"

"No. Just visiting."

"American?"

He nodded. "Born and raised."

"I'm from Canada. It's a different world than this place. I'm used to things moving quickly. Everything in Scotland is slow as molasses."

The man behind the bar said something to one of the customers.

The woman commented again. "And even though everyone speaks English here, I can't understand a word they're saying."

Piero chuckled. "You have a point there. It always takes a little while for my brain to adjust to the accent whenever I go somewhere new. Scotland is no different."

It was his turn to order then, and as soon as he had their drinks in-hand, he turned back toward the table. He nodded to the woman behind him. "Enjoy the rest of your trip."

Felicity's watched over his shoulder before returning her gaze to his face. "You make friends wherever you go…?"

She seemed to be asking him a question, but for the life of him, he couldn't figure out what it was. "It's a blessing and a curse, I suppose."

"Layers."

Her words didn't match her face, but then, women had a habit of being confusing. At least she remembered some of her ramblings from the night before. "We all have them. I'm no exception. Neither—" He pointed his glass of water toward her. "—are you."

She bit her bottom lip before seeming to put aside whatever was on her mind. She reached for her glass and took a drink.

Piero, on the other hand, was still stuck in the conversation. Or at least that last part where she'd bitten her lip. It didn't take much these days to draw his attention to her mouth, and with each passing day, it looked more and more kissable. He could never quite figure out, though, if she felt the same way.

Would she welcome a kiss? He told her he'd wait, but waiting was harder than he'd anticipated. Maybe she didn't remember that conversation…

CHAPTER TWENTY-FOUR

THEY STOPPED AT A COUPLE of shops after lunch as Felicity tried to shake the image of Piero flirting with that woman at the pub.

She picked up a sun hat. They'd decided to go visit a walking path out on a nearby moor. The land, they'd been told, had recently passed out of family hands. While the new owners hadn't developed the land, they had established a walking path and would let tourists pay to enjoy a mapped excursion on the Scottish moors.

"This is different than I imagined." Too many gothic novels while she'd been in high school had given her a very clear mental image of what a Scottish moor ought to look like.

"Scotland has a lot of moors. I don't imagine they all look the same."

"Sure, but... Fields of heather? I expected that, at least."

"I think it blooms in the fall. We're too early. Besides, I'm allergic." Piero swept his arm out, encompassing the wild moor. "You wouldn't get me out here for a walk if the heather were in full bloom."

"Allergic? To Scotland's legendary flower?"

"I can't be the only person in the world who's allergic to heather."

"Maybe not, but you have to know how funny that sounds." She bit back a laugh.

"Would it be even funnier if one of my brothers ended up marrying someone named Heather?"

"Or gives the name to a daughter."

"They both know I'm allergic."

"Maybe they'd do it just to spite you."

Piero chuckled as he shook his head. "I never would have suspected you have such a mean streak hidden behind that enchanting smile."

"You're just trying to change the subject."

"Anything to stop you from laughing at me."

"I was laughing with you."

Piero reached for her hand, and she let him take it.

She liked the way he held her hand. Felicity had never thought of herself as physically affectionate, but whenever Piero touched her — whether it was his hand on her back, a tug at her elbow, or his hand enveloping hers — she realized that maybe her prior indifference to physical affection had little to do with her and everything to do with the person doing the touching.

Piero was different. In all the right ways.

A few minutes later, the man in question cleared his throat. "I know I said I'd wait…"

Uh-oh.

"I still intend to give you time. I just wondered if you could give me an ETA."

He wanted to have *the talk* again.

"Or an estimate. Some kind of timeline, so I'll know…"

Felicity glanced down at their hands, fingers entwined. She could so easily drop his and break the contact. Part of her wanted to. She didn't like these kinds of conversations. They made her uncomfortable in a breaking-out-in-hives kind of way. They're hands looked so good together, though. *So right.*

And, somehow, it seemed like being uncomfortable with Piero was a whole lot better than being comfortable without him.

And that meant telling the truth. Not just to him. To herself, too.

Felicity pulled in a lungful of air and held it for a second. "I might have a problem with jealousy."

Piero's steps faltered, and he came to a stop as he let go of her hand. "Jealousy?"

She nodded.

"I don't understand. Have I given you a reason to be jealous?"

Felicity knotted her fingers together. "The woman at the bar…"

His eyebrows drew together. "What woman? What bar?"

"At lunch. You went to get our drinks. You were laughing with a woman."

He shook his head. "I'm drawing a blank. Today?"

She bit her lip. "She had curly brown hair, a touristy plaid shirt, and khaki shorts. She was behind you in line."

His eyes widened. "Her? She's from Canada. I'm pretty sure I saw her go back to a table with a man and kids — her husband and children, I assumed — she made a joke about how even though people in Scotland speak English, she can't understand them. It was just chit-chat. The kind people make when they're stuck together."

Though it made no sense, her insecurity made her want to cling to him all that more tightly. It was as though the more she doubted him, the more she needed him, and the more she feared losing him. That wasn't who she wanted to be, though. She didn't want to be the person who clung to a man because she was afraid of who she might be without him. Yet here she was, besieged with emotions she struggled to identify and with an image of herself that she wished she'd never seen. "That's what I told myself — that it was innocent. I haven't been able to shake the image, though, and every time it flashes through my brain, I get more upset."

"Have you been jealous the last three days? On the job? Because if you're jealous over a chance encounter in a pub, how can you handle me working with models day in and day out?" Heat colored his voice and punctuated his words.

She'd done it now. He was finally going to get angry over all her silly insecurities. Because that's what they were, after all, weren't they? She was insecure, just like her mom had always said. How had she caught the interest of a guy like Piero? How could she possibly keep that interest?

"I'm nothing like the women you normally date."

"Which probably explains why you're the only woman I've ever broken my two-date rule for."

"I'm nothing special. I don't understand why you're still with me. Or how I'm supposed to prevent you from getting bored with me. I just don't..."

"Stop thinking. You don't keep my interest by doing something. You keep it by being you. You're the one I fell for. You're the person who lit my soul on fire the moment I first noticed you. You're the one I think about all the time. You. No one else."

"I want to trust my heart."

"Then why don't you?"

"Because every time I close my eyes, I remember every ugly thought I ever had about Piero the Playboy."

"Like?"

"He goes through more women in a week than I've gone through men in a lifetime."

He cupped her face in his hands and looked her in the eye. "Not since you. There hasn't been anyone since you. Not a single date. Not a single flirtation. And you have to know I never did anything with those women. I was just a guy on their arm to make them more attractive, unattainable, and sought after. They used me, and I used them."

Against her will, tears began to pool in the corners of her eyes.

"Those women were my armor. They protected me from getting involved with anyone. There was never anything to those relationships — if you can even call them relationships. Everybody knew it, too. That was my reputation, and it kept me safe. I didn't have to open my heart or care too deeply about anybody if everyone knew I wasn't interested in a real relationship."

A tear spilled over. "Then what changed?"

"You're killing me here. Please don't cry. You're the reason I changed. Because you changed everything for me. You made me want more, and that forced me to finally listen to what God had been saying to me all along."

She pulled away from him and wiped her eyes. "Which was?"

"He's always had more for me than a superficial life. I just wasn't interested in listening to Him on the subject until now. It was kind of a two-by-four-upside-the-head moment between me and God. That night in Paris when I went for a walk…"

Laps around the hotel. She remembered him talking about it, but she'd never really pushed to know what it had been about.

"Maybe you need to have your own time to walk with God."

"What do you mean?"

"I've poured my heart out to you. More than once, if I recall. But you don't seem terribly invested in cutting me a break."

"How do you mean?"

"You're going to have to decide whether or not you can trust me." He reached down and plucked a piece of grass from the ground.

"You practically ooze sex appeal. Every time I think I've come to terms with that, something happens to shift my perception, and I start to doubt again."

"I made my bed, and now I need to lie in it. I get that. But you need to decide whether or not you're willing to give me a chance. We can't spend our entire relationship circling back to my past and reputation. We have no future if you can't get past what you thought of me once upon a time."

He looked at her then, a piercing stare that penetrated all the way down to heart and soul. "Either give me hope, or cut me loose. But don't keep yanking me back and forth."

"I never meant…"

He dropped the piece of grass, reached for her hand, and pulled her close enough to wrap in a hug. "I know. But you need to sort it out. I can't do that for you."

CHAPTER TWENTY-FIVE

PIERO NEVER SHOULD HAVE HUGGED her. The drive back to the hotel was too silent. And Felicity insisted on keeping that sun hat on.

She was hiding. He was smart enough to figure that out. He just wished she didn't feel the need to hide from him.

"Remember—" Felicity's voice was tentative, as though she were testing the force of the air around her. "—how I told you that you wouldn't have liked me if we'd met back on any of those earlier shoots?"

He nodded before realizing she wasn't even looking at him. "Yes. I remember."

"I used to have a real problem with judgment. I judged people all the time. God straightened me out, though. Or so I thought."

Piero kept both hands on the wheel, ignoring the urge to reach over and take her hand in his.

"I thought I'd moved past that, but as I look at everything I've thought and felt since you first noticed me, I can see that's not true.

I've fallen back into that same trap. Only, because I thought I'd become immune to it, I didn't see it. I blinded myself to my own problems and blamed everyone else instead."

She was being too hard on herself. Then again... He didn't want her to be hurting over this, but that wasn't really his call. If God was showing her something about herself that needed to change, who was he to tell her she shouldn't worry so much about it?

"Somewhere along the way, I put grace on a high shelf, somewhere I can't reach without a step stool, and I brought judgment down and put it front and center where I could easily get to it."

She seemed to be waiting for him to say something, but his usual eloquence escaped him. "I can see how that would be a problem."

"I haven't been seeing you through the eyes of Christ, which is really what grace is, after all. I've been seeing you through my own worldly eyes. I've been projecting my insecurities onto you and then judging you for whatever wrongs those insecurities conjured up. I haven't been fair to you, and I owe you an apology for that."

He finally reached for her hand, giving it a squeeze. "Apology accepted. I'm not perfect, either, though. Relationships are hard. They force us to look at ourselves in ways we would rather avoid."

"The thing is, I can't promise that this won't happen again. I thought I'd beaten the whole judgment thing, but I was wrong. This might be something that rears its ugly head for the rest of my life. I don't know. I've been giving you mixed signals, and I'm sorry for that. It might keep happening, though, and I..."

Her hat was pulled down even further than before, but it couldn't hide the way she wiped her eyes.

"...I think it's best if we part ways. I don't want to keep doing this to you."

Piero was a man of action. Sitting idly by wasn't something he'd ever been good at, even as a child. He pulled the rental car off the side of the road and got out.

Somewhere between the late lunch and their time spent talking out on the moor, dusk had fallen. This might not be the perfect time or place, but he could work with the tools he had at hand.

He opened Felicity's door and took her hand. She got out of the car without complaint, but she wouldn't look at him.

"Felicity von Wolff, I'd like to kiss you. I don't think you can make a choice like this without being properly informed. You need to collect all the evidence before you can make a decision this monumental."

"I don't know…"

"I won't kiss you against your will, but I think you owe both of us a chance to see what we'd be missing if you end this right now."

The words that came out of her mouth contradicted her shaking head. "All right."

He tugged the hat off her head and tossed it onto the passenger seat. Her blue eyes were luminous in the fading light. He could stare into them forever…if he didn't have more important things to do.

Never had so much ridden on a single kiss.

He leaned in, loosely cupped the back of her neck, and kissed her.

I love you.

Where had that thought come from? Could he…?

His lips moved over hers. While he'd intended to make it a kiss she'd never forget, he hadn't realized how intoxicating her mouth would be. Or how addictive. Piero poured all his feelings into that single kiss — all his love, passion, confusion, and even hurt. Everything. Time wasn't a concept that belonged in a kiss, nor was the passing of it something to be thought about when in the arms of the woman he loved.

Because love her he did. He wouldn't deny it. Yes, it was too fast. No, they hadn't known each other nearly long enough. Yes, they still had a lot to work through. But love? Oh yes. With every fiber of his being, he loved this woman who had captivated his heart and commanded his attention.

Somewhere along the way, her hands had encircled his neck, pulling him closer.

He pulled away from the kiss, head spinning, but stayed within the comfort of her embrace. Piero rested his forehead against hers while his lungs fought his heart for control over his ability to breathe.

His heart eventually slowed to a steady, racing beat, and his lungs once again pulled in the life-giving oxygen they needed.

Love? Yes. The reality of it caused all sorts of crazy reactions. Like the burning desire to never let her speak again. If she didn't talk, she couldn't send him away, couldn't end this thing they had growing between them.

That wasn't the right choice, though. It would never be the right one, either. He owed her — owed both of them — more than that.

"End it if you must, but at least now you know what you're ending."

He brushed his lips against her forehead as she released him from her arms.

CHAPTER TWENTY-SIX

END IT IF YOU MUST.

Ending it couldn't have been further from Felicity's mind if she'd stuck the idea into a rocket and blasted it into outer space.

That kiss…

She couldn't make a decision based on a kiss.

But still… Wow.

Piero was once again behind the wheel. There was no talk of dinner or seeing each other the next day. In fact, there was no talk at all. He drove in silence.

Not that she minded. Felicity was so lost in her own thoughts that she couldn't have held up a conversation if she'd tried.

People shouldn't be allowed to kiss like that. Could they make a law against kissing? Because, if they could…

What was going on with her? Was it getting close to that time of the month? Because her emotions were all over the place. She had a split personality when it came to Piero. She enjoyed his company. She liked his laugh. She loved listening to him talk

about his family and his dreams for the future. She just didn't...
She didn't like how she felt inside when the doubts crept in. She
got all twisted up until she didn't recognize herself.

She was an independent woman. A strong, independent,
resourceful woman, who had been standing on her own two feet
for a good, long while. But every time she started to doubt Piero's
affections for her, she turned into a simpering school girl, who felt
crushed under the weight of unreturned affection.

Felicity cared what Piero thought of her, more than she wanted
to. That was part of the problem. She gripped the seatbelt over her
chest as she tried to sort through the puzzling maze she'd made for
herself. She knew who she was in Christ, and that should be all
that mattered to her. Her insecurities, though, had tricked her into
caring too much about what Piero thought. Then, whenever she
allowed herself to doubt his affections, she doubted herself. She
was becoming... obnoxious. She was turning into one of those
women who constantly sought the approval of the man in her life.

She pitied women like that. How had she allowed herself to
become one?

Piero started humming softly. The sound was loud enough to
register in the recesses of her mind but too quiet to distract Felicity
from her racing thoughts.

Something had shifted in her soul when he'd kissed her. It was
as though all the pieces — the ones from forever-ago and the ones
yet to come — had fallen into place. Yet, still, she struggled to
trust it. So much of what was swirling around inside of her didn't
make sense, and she liked things to make sense.

"Beautiful night." His words intruded on her thoughts.

She glanced out the window. "Yes, it is."

"No, the song. It's Bella Notte. Beautiful Night."

"Oh." Heat climbed her neck. "I thought you were saying..."

"It's not even a real Italian song. It was written in English for a cartoon. Yet it's famous the world over. Everybody knows *bella notte* means *beautiful night*."

Piero talked more than most men, but he rarely said something without meaning or purpose. "Are you getting to the point?"

"Things aren't always what they seem. Sometimes we get so used to hearing something that we forget to stop and question it, to dig deeper."

She turned enough to watch his profile as he talked.

"We think things are supposed to be a certain way because that's what we've been told. Some people might think chili is always spicy, and others might think relationships are always easy. Very few things in this life are always anything, though. Chili is spicy sometimes and mild other times. Relationships are easy sometimes and hard at other times. Very few things worth having are going to be easy all the time."

"You got all that from a song that barely has two stanzas?"

He chuckled. "So you know the song?"

"I grew up as a girl in America. I think knowing "Bella Notte" is required. And I think you're stretching to find that much meaning in it."

He shrugged one shoulder. "Probably. You were thinking hard, though. I wanted to distract you before your brain overheated."

Felicity shook her head. That man… "What does a long-term relationship look like to you?"

His fingers flexed on the steering wheel. "Grace and forgiveness. When two people come together, they're both going to fail and fall. That's human nature. It happens. But being in a relationship together — whether it's related by blood or by choice — requires that both parties forgive and move forward. As long as both parties continue to grow closer to God, they'll grow closer to each other, too."

"Failure and falling."

"Followed by grace and forgiveness."

"You make it sound so simple."

"It's not. It's hard work. My parents had a good marriage, but they worked at it. I didn't understand when I was younger. My mom was a lot like me, though. She was strong-willed and liked to do her own thing. That's pretty much what landed her in America for college. A pinch of following God's will mixed with a whole lot of rebelling against the family. My dad was her opposite in so many ways. They fell in love, though, and God blessed their union. It didn't last long enough, but both their lives were richer for it."

Piero's voice warmed whenever he talked about his folks or his brothers. It did the same for his cousins, but to a lesser extent. He really did love his family.

"What's your dad like?"

"Like you in some ways. I'm pretty sure that proposing to my mom was the first impulsive thing he'd ever done in his life. He never regretted it, though."

Boy, did he ever have her pegged. "It's true. I like to think things through and know where I'm going."

"Sometimes, though, you have to take a leap. Sometimes God asks you to jump in with both feet even though you have no idea where you're going to land."

God wouldn't ask that of her. Would He…?

CHAPTER TWENTY-SEVEN

COULD HE LAY HIMSELF BARE and invite more rejection? A guy could only be expected to take so much on any given day. And yet... He was already all in. There was no point in pretending otherwise.

"Are you willing to put the insecurity and judgement behind you, along with my past and reputation, and go with me to Italy?"

She winced a little, but she didn't flinch. "September, right?"

"If you want to get to know the real me, who I am underneath the charm and polish that I know you adore, what better way? Meet Nonna, my brothers, and my cousins all in one shot. Hear all the embarrassing childhood stories. By the time we're done in Tuscany, you'll know more about me than pretty much anyone on earth who isn't already related to me."

"I want to say yes." She covered her mouth as soon as she uttered the words, a sure sign that she hadn't meant to say it out loud.

"You can stay at the family villa. You'll love it there."

Her faced paled in the moonlight. "I don't know about that…"

"Nonna will insist. Her feelings will be hurt if you try to stay elsewhere." He winked at her. "Separate rooms, of course. Not that I'd do it differently, but trust me. Nobody wants to incur the wrath of Nonna."

"You make her sound so… inviting."

He laughed. Hopefully she wouldn't notice he didn't mean it. He had way too much riding on her answer to find humor in anything at the moment. "Come with me. See where I come from."

"I thought you grew up in Texas."

"And I live in DC. My roots, though? They're buried deep in the Tuscan countryside. That place… It's my legacy. Which sounds lame when I say it out loud, but still. It's a legacy I want to pass on to my children someday."

Felicity looked away before returning her gaze to his. "I have some issues I need to work through. Clearly."

"Sure. So do I. Can't we work on them together, though? Between the two of us, we should have a pretty healthy variety of issues."

"Don't you want to wait to make sure I'm not going to turn into a green-eyed monster every time you speak to another woman?"

He tapped his chest right over his heart. "In here, I know this is right. Yes, we have some things to work through, but everything in me says you're the one God has for me. So why not go for it? Why not leap into the unknown? As long as we're both trusting God, can't we trust that He'll catch us?"

"There's that T-word again. Trust."

At least she hadn't gotten hung up on the *you're the one God has for me* part. Some women might've dug in their heels over that one. Despite her pretty fierce independence, that's not what had snagged Felicity's attention, though. Trust. Hm. There was a lesson in there somewhere. "Yeah. I guess we do keep coming back to that. But for the record, you've never turned into a monster."

"I don't want to be clingy, and when I get jealous, it makes me feel clingy. I don't like the person I become when that happens."

"Then change, and tell me what I can do to help you change. We can support each other, you know. We can help each other to be better versions of ourselves."

They had managed to move a whopping ten feet toward the hotel's entrance. Piero took her hand in his and ran his thumb along the backs of her fingers. He didn't want to let go. "What do you say? Is this going to be our *bella notte?*"

She dropped her gaze, and he could sense the rejection coming. He'd pushed too hard, too fast. He'd let his fear of losing her push her away.

Then she tilted her head back and stared into his eyes.

And she stole his breath away.

A lifetime of laughter and never-a-dull-moment shone in her bottomless pools of blue. Her lips barely moved, but he heard every syllable. "Bella notte."

Heart pounding, he drew her close and kissed her, this time with joy instead of desperation, with hope instead of fear.

He was taking her to meet his grandmother. His Italian grandmother. She didn't realize it yet, but that was practically a wedding proposal.

And she'd said yes.

She loved him. She might not be ready to say it. She might not even know it. She loved him, though, and he savored the taste of that love on her lips.

Felicity ended their kiss and stepped away. She kept her hand in his, though. Baby steps.

"So what made you decide?" Of all the rambling things he'd said that evening — on the moor, in the car, and in the parking lot

— which had been the right thing to say?

"The humming. Definitely the humming."

Of course. The humming.

THE END

AUTHOR'S NOTE

Thank you for taking the time to read *Bella Notte*. I hope you enjoyed Piero and Felicity's story. I loved getting to know Piero the Playboy and Felicity, the woman who wanted nothing to do with him. I believe that too many of us hide from the people around us because we don't want to let them get too close. Felicity hid behind her job as the invisible makeup artist while Piero hid behind his two-date rule and the larger-than-life persona he had created for himself. If you're hiding behind something today, I hope you'll consider putting it aside and letting people get to know your heart.

If you can, please take a minute to tell others about *Bella Notte* by leaving a review on Amazon and Goodreads. I wouldn't mind if you told all your friends about it, too. Or took out an ad in your local paper… although that might get costly. In all seriousness, though, reviews are golden, and I appreciate every single one of them.

Thank you so much!

If you'd like to receive information on new releases, cover reveals, and writing news, please sign up for my newsletter.

ACKNOWLEDGEMENTS

As any writer will tell you, gratitude is a way of life in this line of work. I am beyond thankful that God gives me stories to share and the words with which to tell them. He has allowed me to do something I love, and it's a blessing every single day. Writing isn't a solitary journey, though, and I want to thank the people who have helped pull this story together and make it shine.

Thank you to everyone who cheered me on while catching all my dangling modifiers and missing antecedents: Elizabeth Maddrey, Shari Schroeder, and Kay Springsteen. You're each invaluable.

I also need to give a shout-out to Sarah Hamaker and Pam Green for talking about Paris in such a way that it came alive for me and to Pam, also, for fixing the many ways I managed to butcher the French language. I would also like to thank Marta Aldrighetti for correcting my Italian. If there are any remaining mistakes — in French, Italian, *or* English — trust me, they are all mine.

A TUSCAN LEGACY

THAT'S AMORE
Book 1 by Marion Ueckermann

LUNA ROSA
Book 2 by Elizabeth Maddrey

RAPSODIA
Book 3 by Alexa Verde

TI AMO
Book 4 by Marion Ueckermann

LA FIAMMA SACRA
Book 5 by Clare Revell

BELLA NOTTE
Book 6 by Heather Gray

SOLO TU
Book 7 by Narelle Atkins

DOLCE VITA
Book 8 by Autumn Macarthur

LA RISPOSTA
Book 9 by Autumn Macarthur

SOLO TU
by Narelle Atkins

Home means everything to Sienna Rossi.

Four years ago, Sienna defied her father by moving to Australia to obtain her teaching qualifications. Her grand plan is shaken by her father's unexpected death and a trip back to Tuscany for her grandmother's eightieth birthday where she renews her close bond with her sister, Alessa.

Teacher Dave Maxwell likes the freedom of his nomadic lifestyle. He works contract-to-contract, moving to different high schools around Australia. He's in Sydney for a season, caring for his grandma while his aunt is on an extended overseas vacation.

Back in Sydney, Sienna moves in with her Aussie cousins and starts her first teaching job, torn between her dream for a future in Australia and her longing for home. Sienna and Dave work at the same school, attend the same church, and quickly become friends. They are drawn together by circumstances and an undeniable attraction.

But their idyllic time together is temporary. Can the girl from Tuscany and the boy from Australia risk everything for love?

EXCERPT

HER FIFTH AUTUMN IN AUSTRALIA wasn't ending the way she'd planned.

Sienna Rossi jumped to the left, almost tumbling onto the soft Clontarf Beach sand. A soccer ball flew past and landed in the shallow water. A young family of five played ball together and a little girl giggled, clinging to her father's shoulders.

Sienna regained her balance, a familiar yearning infusing her heart. She longed to be that little girl, delighting in her father's attention. She longed to wind back the years and spend more time with her father and siblings. And she longed for a few more days, or even a few moments, with her Papà. But he was gone.

"Sienna!"

Sienna spun around, her heels digging into the sand.

Her cousin Billie stood twenty feet away with her husband, Zach. "We're organizing the teams. Can you wait here?"

"Sure." Beach cricket. The fun Aussie tradition Sienna had grown to love was next on her Saturday afternoon agenda.

A wind gust blew fine grains of golden sand over her bare arms and legs. Her ponytail anchored her baseball cap in place and sunglasses protected her eyes. In Sydney, it wasn't unusual to wear shorts and t-shirts in late May.

Last week she'd worn summer clothing at the *Italiano* beach near the Amalfi Coast guest house where Mammà's parents lived. Nonna Crisanti had given Sienna two birthday gifts to bring back to Australia. Handmade gifts Nonna Crisanti had chosen for her sisters who'd taken care of Sienna during her time in Australia.

Sienna had visited Nonna Rossi in Tuscany at the end of April. The whole family had returned to Villa Rossi for Nonna's eightieth birthday party. Sienna had met Rachel, the cousin she'd never known existed. Family drama and intrigue were ongoing in the Rossi family. Sienna preferred to ignore it all. Her memories of growing up in Tuscany were bittersweet.

Billie walked hand-in-hand across the park with Zach. Family gatherings, including Sienna's Aussie-Italian family on Mammà's side, congregated in groups on the grass. Zach had planned a game of beach cricket with Dave, his friend from church, and Dave's family.

Dave Maxwell. Billie had told her all about him. In detail. He'd fast gained eligible bachelor status in Billie's eyes. How Billie knew so much when she'd only known him four months was beyond Sienna's understanding.

Dave was a regular at Beachside Community Church, and a teacher at the local high school where Sienna had been hired as a languages teacher on a short-term contract. Billie had seen this as fate, that Sienna and Dave were destined to be a perfect match. Sienna had seen it as a logical coincidence. Over a thousand students attended the high school, and it had a large teaching staff.

Sienna untwisted the tangles in her ponytail then tossed it back over her shoulder. Her hair needed a trim before she started her new job on Tuesday. To save money she'd ask her hairdresser cousin, Jodie, to cut her hair.

Two trips back home to Tuscany this year had decimated her savings. She'd lost her retail job in January, after requesting leave to attend her father's funeral. She couldn't work full-time until her new visa came through, and she'd only picked up occasional days of casual teaching from February to April.

The picnic lunch, provided by her sweet elderly aunts who shared May birthdays, had turned her thoughts to home. Mortadella, salami, cheese, olives. Mouth-watering *Italiano* deli food and animated conversations in her native tongue with an Aussie twang had increased her yearning for Villa Rossi. At least her most recent trip home had been a celebration rather than a time of grief and mourning.

Billie returned with a tall man, his face shaded by a baseball cap. Sienna's gaze was drawn to his muscular chest covered by a fitted red t-shirt and long legs beneath knee length running shorts. He must be Dave.

Billie made the introductions and offered an excuse to leave them. Alone.

162

Dave extended his hand, his eyes hidden by wrap-around sunglasses. "Sienna, good to meet you."

She shook his hand, his palm soft and grip strong. Reassuring.

"Nice to meet you, Dave." Her words sounded clipped and cautious to her discerning ear, as if she wasn't a fluent speaker of English and three other languages.

He grinned. "I like your accent. Billie has told me a lot about you."

Mamma mia! Sienna pushed her sunglasses further up the bridge of her nose, drawing attention to her least-favorite feature.

Dave appeared at ease, as if unaware of her discomfit. He removed his sunglasses and wiped the lens on a corner of his t-shirt, revealing a flat strip of toned stomach above his waistband.

She whipped up her head. *Messa a fuoco.* Think. Fast. "Do you play cricket?"

His hazel eyes held glints of yellow. "My favorite sport."

"Are you any good?"

"You'll soon find out."

She nodded, guessing he was a brilliant player. Her limited cricket experience included a few indoor cricket competitions at university and social games with friends and family.

He adjusted the strap of his backpack, and slung it over his broad shoulder. "I'm glad we had a chance to meet before Tuesday."

"Me too." She dragged her teeth over her lower lip. "My first teaching gig for longer than a few days. No pressure, hey?"

"You'll be fine. The girls in your staffroom can't wait for you to start."

"I heard the baby arrived early."

"By six weeks, but it's all good. Mum and bub are doing well."

"I'm glad."

He slipped his sunglasses back on. "Billie said you're moving to

Beachside Community Church."

"*Si.*" A practical decision she'd made a few days ago. "Beachside is closer to home."

"You're living in Manly, right?"

"I've just moved into a brand-new apartment with my cousins."

"Whereabouts?"

"Near Little Manly Beach."

"The new high-rise tower with the café downstairs."

"That's the one. You know it?"

"I live up the road."

She sucked in a shallow breath. Dave was her neighbor. An important detail Billie had neglected to mention.

Billie and Zach waved them over to a patch of grass further along the beach. A group had gathered around them, including a few kids.

Dave tipped his head in their direction. "It looks like it's game on."

"Yes." She fell into step beside him. "Who's playing from your family?"

"My older brother and uncle and a couple of cousins. It looks like we'll have a few ring-ins to make up the numbers."

She scrunched her nose. "Ring-ins?"

"Random people who join in. You haven't heard that expression?"

"If I have, I don't remember."

"It must get confusing. You speak a few languages, right?"

"Only four."

"Only four." A playful tone underpinned his words. "I know you're teaching Italian and French."

"And Spanish."

His grin revealed a cute dimple in his chin. "I'll have to take you to Europe as my tour guide."

164

Heat rushed up her neck, warming her face. The thought of being his personal tour guide . . .

Focus. Concentrate. Remember how to speak English. "That's my *sorellina's* job."

"Your *sorellina?*"

"My little sister."

"She's a tour guide."

"In Roma. Rome." Alessa's teasing would be relentless if she'd heard this conversation.

"Have you seen the Catacombs?" Dave asked.

"*Si.* I was there a few weeks ago."

"I've been to Paris, but I want to see the Catacombs in Rome."

"Definitely worth a visit. Do you speak many languages?"

"Very poor French. Embarrassingly poor. You don't want to hear it."

She chuckled, his honesty disarming. "You teach English, right?"

"English I can do, but I'm teaching only one English class this year. History and geography are my focus."

He was down-to-earth and could laugh at himself. An appealing trait. She liked him. Probably too much.

ABOUT HEATHER GRAY

Heather Gray loves coffee, God, her family, and laughter — not necessarily in that order! She writes approachable characters who, through the highs and lows of life, find a way to love God, embrace each day, and laugh out loud right along with her. Her books almost always include someone who's infatuated with coffee, too. Some things just can't be helped. Heather delights in creating characters who, like her, have their share of faults and foibles, characters who are flawed…but loved anyway.

Please visit Heather's website for more of her books.
www.heathergraywriting.com

OTHER TITLES BY HEATHER GRAY

Informal Romance
contemporary Christian romance
An Informal Christmas (Book 1)
An Informal Arrangement (Book 2)
An Informal Introduction (Book 3)
An Informal Date (Book 4)
An Informal Affair (Book 5)

Rainbow Falls
contemporary Christian romance
Skye (coming summer 2018)
Sunny (coming winter 2018)
Rose (coming spring 2019)

Trinity Community Church Romance
contemporary Christian romance
Definitely (coming fall 2018
Fantastic (coming spring 2019)

Regency Refuge
regency historical Christian romance
His Saving Grace (Book 1)
Jackal (Book 2)
Queen (Book 3)

Stand-Alone Novels
contemporary Christian romance
Ten Million Reasons
Nowhere for Christmas

Printed in Great Britain
by Amazon

18080298R00099